BARBARA COMBS WILLIAMS

THE DARKEST GREY
MATTOCK FAMILY SAGA
BOOK 3

REMEMBER TOO DESIGN © 201

A REMEMBER TOO DESIGN

ACKNOWLEDGEMENT

I want to thank so many people for helping me make this third novel *The Darkest Grey* possible. There is, of course, my wonderful husband Heyward, who without his influence these 40+ years I never would have started writing.

Thanks to our daughter Nicole, who gave me so much help with understanding Millennials, Gen Xs, Gen Zs, any other letters, and what makes them tick.

Then, there is my editor/coach/friend Candice L. Davis, who encouraged me to start this publishing business, to get my words out there for you all to read.

Next, is a friend I made through writer networks. Ravyn Wilde, the queen of alien paranormal romance, took me under her wings, and gave me such insight into this business. My writing world has been so much better with her in my corner.

Lastly, I thank you, my readers for hanging in there with me. Thank you for reading all my books, short stories, and poetry.

We all have a voice, maybe we don't speak up as we should. So, I'm going to help you along. This is for all of you, who want to be heard, but never dared.

DEDICATION

Mom, Dad, and brother Robert, miss you guys dearly. You all, are the angel wings on my shoulders. You keep my heart beating...

Thank you all from the bottom of that heart!

Barbara

CHAPTER 1

James "Jimmy" Mattock Jr. had no idea where he was. He had awakened earlier, startled by a clock chiming, and found himself in a foul mood.

Jimmy tried to methodically catalog his body parts. He knew he had a head because it was pounding so severely. He felt his left hand, because he was lying on it, and it hurt with a stinging pain. He felt both legs, and then he sensed the rest of his body, because it all hurt so very badly.

His head felt as if soiled towels had been stuffed into his mouth and pulled out through his nose passing through his brain on the way.

Jimmy had trouble opening his eyes due to the stickiness gluing them together.

His mouth tasted like rotten cabbage with a side of fish head stew thrown in for good measure.

Jimmy's chest burned like a gasoline fire had ignited down his throat. In general, he felt like shit.

He wondered why he was lying on the floor. He was drifting in and out of consciousness, and he thought his mind must be playing tricks with his body because it was difficult to tell what was what.

Why was he on the floor? More precisely he was on top of his expensive Burmese rug. He could see a blurry splash of color pressed up against his face.

Somehow or other, he must have lain down on the rug to take a nap. But even to his fogged mind that assumption didn't sound quite right.

Why would he sleep on his floor when he knew he had a massive king bed, full of comfortable sheets and pillows?

Was he even in his house in Alpharetta? Or had he been kidnapped and hauled away, awaiting some ransom to be paid?

Like a runaway freight train, the truth of his situation came roaring down on him. Then a headache so terrible that to breathe almost killed him, pierced him behind his eyes. He wanted to puke just thinking about the past twelve hours.

The disastrous showdown with Bryan, Chrystal, and her so-called fiancé Tyler rushed through his mind like a crazy vampire movie, where he had not a silver bullet left to his name.

What little sense he had left was locked and targeted on the previous night. Jimmy remembered what his distorted mind told him was his mate Bryan walking out on him when he needed him most.

His daughter Chrystal was furious and childish because he tried to look out for her. She made what he thought at the time were idle threats of disowning him. That was the ultimate betrayal.

And then Chrystal, his one and only walked out of his house with that pitiful excuse for a fiancé, Tyler, looking at him like he would a poisonous snake.

And like a damn fool, he had drunk Kentucky whiskey until there wasn't any more to drink.

His jumbled mind replayed the three a.m. confrontation between him, Bryan, Chrystal, and Tyler.

The two young people had looked to Bryan for guidance as they sat down on the same sofa Jimmy was now lying down beside. As if Bryan held all the answers to Jimmy's behavior, they'd turned their gaze to him for confirmation of what they thought they knew.

Chrystal had caught Jimmy planning to send the pathetic excuse for criminals, Smoke and Duck out to Chrystal's mother's house to hurt Jackie, and her boyfriend Eric.

Truth be told, he had used the same criminals to make an unwanted baby daddy disappear out of Chrystal's life.

Yes he had done all that and more because it was the right thing to do, but he would deny it to his last day on earth, and unfortunately, that day might just be here.

Chrystal had said to Bryan when he tried to intervene, "Thank you so much for always trying to calm daddy down, but right now I want him to talk. I want him to come right on out and tell it all. All the disgusting things he did to hurt Mama and Eric, including working with nasty Smoke and Duck and even skank-ass Nikki. And I want him to tell me exactly how he's going to make this shit right."

As usual, Jimmy denied everything. He spoke to Tyler as if he were a low life and he treated Chrystal like a child, instead of a young mother of three. And Bryan, Jimmy ignored him altogether.

Now, Jimmy remembered Chrystal calling him out, even though he pretended innocence.

She'd jumped up from her seat and cried out, "Daddy, you must think I'm a child. By now even you, should know better."

Tyler gathered her into his arms and hugged her tight. "It's okay, babe. I'm here. It's going to be all right. Everything's going to be all right," said Tyler as he sat Chrystal back down.

Bryan had stared at Jimmy as Tyler tried to console Chrystal. "Well Jim, what do you say to this? Your one and only daughter is distraught because you've betrayed her trust. You have lied, misled her, and broken her heart--you her father, whom she trusted. What do you have to say to make this right?"

Jimmy had snorted and shook his head. He'd rolled his eyes at Bryan. Jimmy was one word away from telling everyone to go to hell.

"Mr. Mattock," said Tyler, "Chrystal has told me how much she loves you and believe me I'm not trying to come between you two. But as you can see,

5

Chrystal has been hurt so badly by all this that I had to agree with her. Maybe she and you need a break from each other. Enough time to heal, if such a thing is possible. I think --"

"Look here, Tyson. I don't give a damn what you think," Jimmy had responded. "You're in no position to agree or disagree with Chrystal. Apparently, you're new in the picture. Where have you been all this time? Jade is almost sixteen months old."

"Daddy stop!"

"No! I will not stop. My baby has been struggling all on her own with three children. One of whom is yours. This is the first time I've ever heard of you. So I don't think we need to hear anything from you!"

Jimmy was seething. *How dare this little boy try to tell me what's best for my daughter.*

"Besides, Chrystal has leaned on my help all her life, and I've been totally involved with every one of her children. As a good father and grandfather, I know what's best for them."

Chrystal wiped her eyes and nervously gripped Tyler's hand. "His name is Tyler, not Tyson." She turned to her fiancé. "It's okay. You don't have to explain anything to him. Thank you for trying to make him understand. But I got this." Chrystal gave Tyler a small kiss on the cheek and sat back down.

"Daddy, I want action, not just pretty words. You've hurt so many people. And you wanted to hurt so many more, especially Mama. Why should I believe anything you have to say? As they say, talk is damn cheap. So what are you going to do now?"

Jimmy tried to be glib and give his family flippant answers as he smiled, showing all his teeth.

"Do? I don't know what you mean. I told you all that the situation had been taken care of. Duck and Smoke are no longer working for me. So that's that."

Jimmy rolled his eyes at them as if they were stupid to think anything else.

Bryan had looked at him with hurt in his eyes and for a moment Jimmy felt a small degree of anxiety. But that was quickly replaced with anger as Chrystal continued to beat him up with her verbal abuse.

She had shaken her head at him, as if she were talking to one of her small children. "I see. So do you think that's good enough? You have to be kidding me. This is so messed up. I can't believe you got the nerve to stand there and tell us this bullshit. You must believe we're the craziest people on earth if you think we would believe these lies."

By that time, Jimmy was thoroughly finished with all of them. His temper flared and his mouth took on a will of its own, running full blast without a thought to the consequences of his words.

"Your precious mother and her homophobic boyfriend are safe from me. I said I was sorry. I'm through with this damn conversation already. I really don't want to hear anymore from you or Bryan. You are all dismissed."

He continued to smile as he stood up and moved to the liquor cabinet to refill his drink. There he drank whiskey until the light of day seeped through his windows.

But now, Jimmy wasn't sure who he despised the most, as he lay in excruciating pain on his high-priced carpet. There was of course, his dictator of a father, James Mattock Sr., for whom he was named.

Jimmy called him spawn of Satan. Demon God, Beelzebub. The originator of all lies and pain, evil personified, torturer of innocents and so on, and so on.

When Jimmy was a child, his father had made Jimmy's life a living hell. Nothing he ever did met the senior Mattock's list of standards. If he turned right, his father wanted left. If he studied chemistry, his father wanted him to study political science. If he expressed any sort of emotion, his father called him weak and a mama's boy.

And now, here he was a grown man with children and grandchildren of his own, and still he felt as insecure as a teenaged boy on his first date when it came to his relationship with his father.

That selfsame man had come to town just to mess with Jimmy's head, dragging his fragile wife, Jimmy's mother, with him, just to make his son look small and insignificant to his own children. Just to make him feel weak and like a failure.

James Sr. humiliated Jimmy by handing out to Chrystal and Royce big globs of money, like manna from heaven, trying successfully to buy their love and allegiance.

This man, his father would forever be a demon, a devil, the satanic embodiment of all the evil in the world. Jimmy's hatred towards men like James Mattock Sr. was the life blood that pumped through his veins.

Then again there was the woman he blamed his own downfall on, his ex-wife, Jackie. She came in almost tied for first place on his list of most hated. She was the bitch who sang her death song as she twisted the sharpest blade against his jugular. She, who he specifically picked for her naivety, or so he'd thought.

She'd beguiled him and then passed off the bastard boy-child as his. For twenty-five years, she had been the biggest spike in his side. He couldn't let her win. He had too much at stake to let that happen.

Or maybe he should heap all his suffering onto his mate Bryan. Bryan, who flashed a trustworthy smile, but thoroughly stabbed Jimmy in his heart as he stroked his arm. Bryan, on whom he lavished all the material goods a man could want. Cars, condos, jewelry, money, and gourmet wines and food. Bryan who Jimmy placed upon a pedestal as his true heartmate.

A random college meeting that turned into a lifetime of togetherness. A thousand and one times, that Bryan, whom he had groomed and perfected, now betrayed him.

Then there was his only daughter by blood or love, Chrystal. Jimmy had planned his life around her and sacrificed his pride for her. He associated with felons and drug-dealing scum just to protect her. He brought her into the bosom of his home even after her whore of a mother corrupted her.

He did all this and more because he loved her as only a father can. But she told him she never wanted to speak to him again in this life or another. She said she was through with him. Chrystal's hatred towards him was the ultimate disloyalty, and it stabbed him clean through his heart.

Her actions were the deadliest poison that burned like acid as it ate through his brain. Chrystal wanted him to apologize and make amends to her mother for his past actions. Really? Was she even sane to think he would do such a thing?

Lastly there was his not-really son Royce, the bastard of another man, about whom Chrystal so hatefully told Jimmy, "Oh my bad. He's really not your flesh and blood, is he? Too bad, he'll just have to do."

Royce had brought it all to a thunderous boil by bringing his accursed biological father into Jimmy's presence. Royce had placed this father down, front and center, pushing Jimmy to the background.

Jimmy still wasn't sure how he really felt about Royce. On one hand, he was proud of the young man's scheming, but on the other side, he had to deal with the disrespect Royce had thrown down like a gauntlet.

Royce had brains and graduated at the top of his engineering class. He also instigated the disgraceful meeting at his wedding to Jessica and brought such chaos into Jimmy's life.

This same Royce was the child genius who had orchestrated Jimmy's downfall right at the wedding reception for him and Jessica.

But most of all, Royce looked just like his blasted biological father, Eric, who schemed his way into Jackie's heart and apparently her body. That was the one thing Jimmy could never forgive him or her for.

He wasn't going to beg any of them for their traitorous love. He didn't need them. They would surely one day need him more, but it would be too late. They were all evil and deceitful and so dead to him.

He had time, so he thought, to muse on his fate. He continued to dream up torturous ways to hurt his estranged family. He wouldn't be happy until he had paid them back a thousand-fold for the pain they caused him.

Jimmy struggled to his back, thinking the pain would lessen. He was wrong of course. Mistaken again, as he had been about most things in his life.

But that wasn't his fault. He was the one who had been wronged. He had been deceived. His own daughter had rejected him and placed others before him. It hurt his pride to think of this truth.

LATER THAT DAY

The ugly cuckoo clock chimed. It was one of the many things he and Bryan had argued over. Jimmy thought it was hideous and forbade Bryan from bringing it into the house.

But Bryan had fallen in love with the thing when he was antique hunting. He thought the clock would bring a touch of 'whimsy' – his words, not Jimmy's-- to the family room.

It was a deep chocolate-colored wooden house. It also had enough trim and frills poking from it to decorate twenty more ugly bird houses.

The nasty, bedraggled bird sprung out on its roost was the dullest yellow he had ever seen. The whole thing reminded Jimmy of something from some dusty sixteen century peasant farmhouse.

He'd allowed the clock in the house after Bryan begged and cried, but only if Bryan could fix the damn thing so it only chimed once every other hour. Jimmy despised it thoroughly, like so many things in his life he had no control over.

From his position on his back, he could just make out the time. It looked like eleven o'clock in the morning. He was glad, now, for the clock's presence. By his rough estimate, he had lain on the floor for almost an hour since he woke up.

He closed his eyes again, taking breaths as deep as possible. That must have been the wrong choice, for the pain reared its head again and sizzled like lightning through his body.

The agony returned to his breastbone. So razor-sharp and stabbing he looked to see if he was impaled on some knife-like object. He wasn't sure how he'd made it to the floor. But there he lay, weakened and still slightly drunk from two or three bottles of whiskey.

Now, pure torture radiated from his chest into his back. It felt as if someone had opened a channel from front to back and poured liquid volcanic fire directly into the pathway. It burned and burned and traveled down into his guts.

He fought back bitter bile that tasted disgustingly of said whiskey, a spoiled and rotten brew that burned his throat and brought water to his eyes. And that was supposed to be the best whiskey money could buy. He should get his money back for that horrid mess. Still, his guts rolled and gurgled.

Jimmy struggled for breath. And every inhale brought a new round of agony. *So this is how it ends, he thought. A damn heart attack takes me out as I lie here on this expensive rug, puking on my shirt. Hmph! It's the one Bryan gave me for Christmas too.*

"The darkest grey, with the old English spelling," Bryan had said pretentiously. It was almost black he'd said. It will complement every color of slacks.

Jimmy had never cared for the color. It did nothing to bring out the chocolate brown of his eyes. It made his skin look washed out and tired. He wondered if it would look good once he died.

To Jimmy, it was a dreary and boring color. Much like his life had become. Was that why he fought so hard to bring discord into everyone's life? Well maybe some excitement was finally about to occur.

Jimmy imagined the scene once his dead and decaying body was found. He had heard the body fouls itself as it slides into death. At least his jeans were also dark. *Maybe it will hide the shit stains,* he moodily thought.

"Oh, my God, my Lord! I'm so sorry, Jim. Please, God take me too. I never should have left you. Please forgive me. I love you so much. Please God, take me instead!"

That of course would be Bryan. Bryan would cry and shudder and put on a good show. He would make eye contact with the others who showed up to gloat and give them fiery looks of disgust. *Bryan will blame each and every one of them for my death.*

Jimmy tried to chuckle as he pictured his absent companion's theatrics. But the pain was intensifying.

"Please, Jim, come back to me. I'll do whatever you want. I'll be there for you. I won't put any of these traitors before you. I understand now. Please forgive me. It's all your fault Chrystal. And you too Royce. You both should be ashamed. Jackie, you did this to Jim. Your hatred is what killed him. I hate all of you! I'll never forgive any of you.

"And you too Mr. Mattock! You came here from Denver with nothing but ugly loathing in your heart to torture my precious Jim. You've never been a good father to my dear Jim. You treated him like a peasant and beat him up daily with your mental abuse. You're the worst demon to ever crawl out of Hades."

Bravo, bravo! Bryan wins the Academy Award for his performance. *Now, let's see.* Maybe Jackie would fall to her knees at my side. Moaning and groaning. She'd probably turn on my father and blame him for his treatment of me.

"Mr. Mattock, you devil. It's your fault. You knew Jimmy was trying to change. You came here with your nasty attitude and ugly ways. You treated Jimmy worse than a dirty mongrel at the curb. You kicked him and punched him with your demands. Oh, Lord! What are we going to do now? Oh Lord, Jimmy's gone!"

Well maybe that's a little too much love for Jackie to express. That's more like Ms. Sylvi, Jackie's mother. *Yes, Ms. Sylvi loves me still. She would pray over my dead body and ask the Lord to save me.*

"Dear Lord, please forgive me for blaming Jimmy for his and Jackie's terrible breakup. Now I know, Lord, that it wasn't his fault. Jackie pushed him too far. She had relations with another man. No good husband could put up with that. Please, Lord, please. Let Jimmy's spirit pass on to the Promised Land and sit at your side. Thank you Lord."

Another deep pain shook Jimmy's body. He moaned, and the bile entered his throat and burned his nasal passages.

Okay, okay, maybe that's too much too for Ms. Sylvi to be thinking. I get your message. But she will miss me. I know she will.

Jimmy started to roll over again and fought back the stabbing pain. He was sweating now and his shirt had big wet stains under the arms and down his back. *I'll just close my eyes and rest and move again later,* he thought.

A ringing cell phone somewhere in the house, woke Jimmy. He slowly opened his eyes. Again, he was able to make out the clock from where he lay. Somehow, the clock now read twelve. To his amazement, an hour had gone by, and he was still lying on the floor—and still alive.

Little did he know, his daughter, Chrystal, was praying for his demise.

CHAPTER 2

Chrystal Marie Mattock sat in her grandmother's kitchen. The house was in a quiet, family-oriented neighborhood in Atlanta. This was the same kitchen that held so many memories of summer days and Christmas mornings. Chrystal had to admit most of those memories were good ones.

Still, it took her a while to slowly raise her head from her hands. Her thoughts were troubled. Again, her young life was going to hell and she felt powerless to stop it.

"Mommy, what's wrong?" That was her oldest child, Jewell. At five, Jewell looked more like a three-year-old. She was small for her age, but she was smart and very observant. She laid her small hand against her mother's face.

"Oh, baby, nothing's wrong. Mommy's just a little tired. I had a long night. My head's hurting.

That's all." Chrystal hugged her daughter to her chest. She loved Jewell as well as her other two children, Oro, and Jade, who were playing happily on the kitchen floor.

"Come here baby, Great-gran got something for you." Chrystal's grandmother, Ms. Sylvi, who was washing dishes at the sink, motioned to Jewell as she put away her dish towel.

Chrystal could tell her grandmother was trying to distract Jewell from her mother's suffering. She gave her grandmother a slight nod, recognizing what she was trying to do.

Ms. Sylvi pulled on Jewell's curly pigtail and Jewell giggled. "Let's get your little brother and sister and go watch some cartoons in the family room. How does that sound? I got some cookies for each one of you too."

Chrystal's fiancé and Jade's father, Tyler, hugged little three-year old Oro and rubbed his head full of shiny, dark curls as he gave him a gentle push in Ms. Sylvi's direction.

Then Tyler reached down and picked up sixteen-month-old Jade from the floor and handed her over to Ms. Sylvi. He gave Jade a tickle under her chin, and she giggled and kissed her dad on his cheek.

"Thank you, Ms. Sylvi," said Tyler. I think that's a great idea. Go ahead Jewell, and Oro too. You guys go on and have some fun. Your mom and I will be along in a little while."

Chrystal watched them all as they made their way to the family room, and then she turned to Tyler. "Thanks bae. I'm trying to get past this, but I feel so sad. And this gray cloudy day isn't helping any." Chrystal tried to give Tyler a smile but her heart just wasn't in it.

She thought back to the last scene with her father. It had hurt her terribly. Jimmy was a monster and only now was it so crystal clear to her that he always had been. She had no forgiveness left in her heart for his terrible actions.

It was a little past noon on an otherwise typical Saturday morning in June. The day had started out sunny, even though Chrystal, Tyler, Bryan, Royce, and Royce's new wife, Jessica, had to meet at Ms. Sylvi's house so early.

The news they brought with them was devastating. It took all the joy from a day that started out so peaceful in Ms. Sylvi's house.

Chrystal's mother Jackie, and her aunt, Nancy, were spending the weekend with their mother, Ms. Sylvi. They were helping to take care of Chrystal's children while she tied up the loose ends of moving.

Chrystal had agreed to move in with her grandmother while she finished nursing school. She and the kids had almost completed the move and were settling in when all hell broke loose, again.

Earlier that same morning, they'd all converged upon Ms. Sylvi's house. Even now, after a few short hours, it was difficult to sort through the latest disaster and face the facts of her father's crazy behavior.

Chrystal had spoken up for Bryan, her father's significant other, after her aunt had cussed Bryan out for what she thought he and Jimmy had done to hurt her sister.

"Please, don't blame Bryan for this," Chrystal had said. "He had nothing to do with this mess daddy has caused. In fact, he tried his best to stop daddy, but you can see it didn't go well. He had to leave that house of horrors. That's why he's here with us now."

Chrystal tried to block the memories, but they continued to beat her up mentally as the clear-as-water images dug deeper into her brain.

Tyler looked at Chrystal, who was still rubbing her forehead. "A penny for your thoughts," he said.

"Although I'm sure I know what they are." He smiled at her across the table.

The sky had turned from sunny to dark gray clouds, threatening summer rain at any moment.

"I was thinking about this morning. I can't bear to sit here and do nothing. I mean, I can't get my head around what daddy has done, and how I went along with him. I hate him so much. I wish he would just disappear."

Chrystal again buried her face in her trembling hands. She was overwhelmed with the despair she tried to hide.

"You didn't know everything he was doing, bae. You are not responsible for what your father has done. He's an adult, and he made the decision to use you and hurt others. It's not your fault. You can't control your dad. And you don't hate him.

You're just disappointed in what he's done. I can't blame you for feeling that way."

Tyler moved around the table to Chrystal's side. He knelt and hugged her around her waist.

Tears threatened to spill as Chrystal continued to think about her part in Jimmy's sordid plans

"I know, but I can't help feeling guilty. He said he did this stuff for me. He said he was trying to protect me. I feel like it's my fault for being such a bitch to Mama. I believed him and all his lies. I believed him because I wanted to blame mama for things that she didn't even do."

She ran her hands distractedly through her thick, dark hair. It had a natural curl pattern that moved with her head as she pushed it around. With a final huff, she blew the offending strains out of her shiny, wet eyes.

Chrystal continued to confess as Tyler rubbed her back and hugged her tighter.

"You know mama and I have an up-and-down sort of relationship. I blamed her for their divorce. I blamed her for keeping Daddy away from me. I thought she was the one doing all this stuff. You know, just trying to hurt me and daddy. I just wanted him to love me but I never knew that Daddy did so much shit to mama. There's no way anybody could've put up with that mess."

Chrystal cried silently on Tyler's shoulder as she continued to relive her conversation with her family in her mind.

She had started by saying, "I'm going to try to tell you all everything that went on. Like I said, I have done some things that I am so ashamed of, but please let me get the whole story out before you say anything."

For half an hour, she told her family everything that had occurred. She shared everything from the disastrous situation with Omar, Oro's father, down to the drug dealing criminals, Smoke and Duck. She told them how Jimmy had confronted her when he found out she was pregnant with Oro, and she'd broken down and told Jimmy what was going on.

The baby's father, Omar, had wanted to take the baby from Chrystal once he found out she was having a boy. Omar didn't want his son treated as an outcast and planned to take him from Chrystal and return to his homeland of Pakistan. He left no doubt he only wanted his son; he didn't need or want Chrystal.

When Jimmy found out the predicament Chrystal was in, he told his daughter he would take care of the situation. Unbeknownst to Chrystal, he schemed with Smoke and Duck to drive Omar out of the country.

Chrystal also mentioned Nikki's part in getting Jimmy in contact with Smoke and Duck in the first place. Nikki had connected Chrystal to Smoke, who called himself a music producer, when Chrystal needed help raising money for nursing school. Smoke was supposed to help her make some quick cash.

Chrystal told her family how she'd agreed to do videos with Smoke to promote various artists' music as a way to earn the extra money. And she finally told everyone how Smoke and Duck really just used her for drug transactions, and Nikki, being childish, and jealous, sabotaged one of the deals.

Nikki had withheld ten thousand dollars from a drug payoff, and Smoke accused Chrystal of taking it. But she and Nikki had managed to pay Smoke back and get out of his place intact--and with the knowledge of Jimmy's betrayal.

After she'd revealed all that shocking news, Chrystal had continued, telling them how she found out from Smoke that Jimmy paid him and Duck to beat up people, and how Jackie and Eric were on his hit list.

She'd concluded with her plea to Jimmy to come clean about his plans to hurt her mother, and how, instead, the conversation had ended with Bryan leaving Jimmy because of his horrifying actions.

Chrystal had shared a lot of what happened, but she did not tell them about her intimate involvement with Smoke. She would forever be ashamed of being used sexually by someone like him. And to her dying day, she hoped Tyler and her family would never find out exactly how big of a fool she had been.

Chrystal had tears in her eyes as she finished sharing her news that morning. Her mother, Chrystal believed, had looked at her with shock and sadness in her eyes. She also believed her aunt Nancy still blamed her personally for Jimmy's action. And her grandmother was stunned into silence by the terrible truth.

For Chrystal, the conversation brought back all the guilt, embarrassment, and remorse she'd felt when her mother Jackie told everyone how Chrystal was conceived. She knew her mother had only done what she did for love.

But why had she, Chrystal, messed up her life so badly? She couldn't figure it out. Compared to her strong mother, Chrystal felt like the biggest failure her parents had ever created, just one huge disappointment.

Her brother Royce's wife, Jessica, had hugged her tightly, but Chrystal only saw pity in the other young woman's eyes.

Poor Bryan had taken the brunt of all their hostilities. She knew he was very sensitive and would probably never recover from the pain and humiliation her family heaped on him.

She couldn't blame her mother anymore for her actions. Instead Chrystal felt pride in how her mother had been able to hold it together for so long. With a man like her father, she was surprised her mother hadn't killed him a long time ago.

Overall, Chrystal felt hopeless and lost. She had trouble believing anything anyone told her, and she knew her family looked at her with doubt in their minds as to the truth of her words.

Chrystal and Tyler were newly engaged and he tried to lift her spirits with his support, but more than anything, she didn't want him to think of her as a slut passed around by criminals.

Their relationship was rocky at times. Being only Jade's dad and not Jewell's or Oro's, would be a lot for any man to take, especially since it was so obvious that no two of the children had the same father.

But Tyler was a good man, and he was trying so hard to be there for Chrystal. Still, even he could only take so much. If he found out about her sexual activity with Smoke, he wouldn't be able to forgive her

She had done these things while she should have been waiting faithfully for Tyler to return from his music tours. He traveled the world, playing his acoustic guitar for big-named singers and he was very good at it. He was making a name for himself in the music industry and trusted her to stand by his side while he was away. If he found out about her betrayal with Smoke, it might break that little trust they'd built together.

Chrystal had believed she was in love far too often, and definitely with the wrong people. In her heart she finally believed she had found the right man to keep her love safe. But now she stood on the edge of a crevice, with a steady wind blowing her towards the darkness below.

Now, just a few hours after she'd revealed so much of her experience to him and her family, Tyler pulled Chrystal up from her chair and hugged her tight, as her mind came back to the present.

"Listen," he said. "I told you. I will never forgive myself for not being here when you needed me most. But most of all, I want you to know my love for you has not changed one bit. I'm here now, and nothing's going to stop us from spending the rest of our lives together as a family."

Chrystal hugged Tyler back and lay her head on his chest. She continued to think about the information she hadn't told him.

If you knew the disgusting things I did with that piece of shit, you wouldn't be holding me so tightly, she thought to herself.

Aloud, her lips only managed to say, "I love you so much." And silently she prayed: *I hope that's enough. Please God, let that be enough.*

CHAPTER 3

Bryan Denveue was packing a bag with clothes from the closet in his Midtown condominium's bedroom.

He needed an escape. He needed to get away from it all. His hands trembled as he picked through last season's trendy summer clothes. But his mind was back in his true home in Alpharetta—with Jim.

It had been several hours since he left his and Jim's house and traveled with Chrystal and Tyler to Ms. Sylvi's home. The last words Jim had spoken to him replayed in his mind even though it all had happened hours ago.

"If you're leaving, then leave, damn it," Jim had told him. "Don't waste my time standing there sniveling and looking like a damn lost bitch mongrel."

Jim's words cut him to the bone. Bryan had looked at Jim and sadly shaken his head, saying the only thing that came into his head.

"I'm so sorry for you Jim, for us. Do you really want me to leave our home?"

Jim had just looked at him, not answering, just staring blankly at his face. Bryan felt as if he was *looking at an evil stranger.*

"Well, I guess this is the end then? But I'm so disappointed in you. I thought you and I . . . I mean, I thought you cared. I don't know what to say anymore."

Even now, Jim's behavior made Bryant's heart ache. He thought he knew this man. All the years they had been together now amounted to much of nothing, except to make Bryant feel old, fat, and unwanted.

He sucked in his belly and tried to straighten his back. He ran his hand over his thinning hair. *Jim has made all my bright red hair go grey and fall out from the stress,* he thought. *And of course his hair is just as dark and pretty as the first day we met.*

Bryan sat on the edge of the bed and relived their first fateful encounter.

Their meeting in college occurred over thirty-five years earlier. The Atlanta University campus was crowded, full of young students when Jim accidentally ran into him in the student quad. That sunny spring day was the first day of their life together.

For Bryan, it was destiny. There was no way it could have been otherwise. He was the only one James Mattock Jr. allowed to call him by his shortened nickname, Jim. This man was everything and a bag of spicy chips to Bryan.

Jim complimented his exuberant style with his quiet, sedate demeanor. They had fun together, and side by side, Bryan believed they'd built a solid, loving relationship.

But now, horrible as it was to admit, Bryan was beyond through with Jim's behavior. The things Jim had done. The number of people he had lied to, and yes, who he'd also made Bryan lie to, made his heart lurch inside his chest.

He'd first found out that Jim was using Duck and Smoke as hit men purely by accident when Duck left Jim a message. Bryan confronted Jim, and Jim practically shoved him away.

Jim had been so angry. For once, Bryan thought Jim might actually do him physical harm. But instead, Jim had laughed it off as if it were a joke. He then played with Bryan's mind by lying to him and continuing to lie to everyone involved.

That had happened several days ago, and Bryan had believed Jim when he agreed to stop his crazy actions. Bryan should have known it wasn't so. He'd begged Jim over and over, until it hurt his own head to hear himself plead. But it did no good. Psychotic behavior had become a way of life to Jim. He had turned into the worst kind of psychopath, a very determined and delusional one.

Their conversation played through his mind again like an old vinyl record.

"Please, for your sake, for all our sakes," he had said, "Let it go. Leave Jackie and Eric alone. They deserve some happiness. You and I deserve some happiness. Don't throw what we have away on petty revenge. Learn to be content with what you have. And please, forget about what you think you don't have. Please do it for me. Do it for us."

Apparently, Jim didn't love him enough because he continued to lie and blame everyone else for his self-made misfortune. And the saddest thing was Bryan still loved him dearly.

Now, Bryan slowly got up from the bed. He walked into his closet and picked through his colorful wardrobe. He was thinking of taking a plane to some faraway tropical island. Resting under an umbrella and drinking exotic cocktails would take his mind off what he'd lost. At least, he hoped it would.

His best clothes were back at the home he shared with Jim in Alpharetta. In this little condo, which Jim had surprised him with, Bryan kept only essentials and last year's clothes.

This condo had turned into a place he could go for a little alone time. A place to regroup and get away from the stressful life of living with Jim.

Over the years Bryan had decorated and redecorated the two bedroom condo. Not surprisingly, it was very fashionable and full of Bryan's flamboyant style.

More than twenty-five years ago, Jim had gifted Bryan with the condo. Of course, back then it was in a little-known area of Atlanta. Now with urban development, it had become one of the premier neighborhoods in Virginia-Highlands.

Jim had purchased the condo a few years before he married Jackie and it served as Bryan and Jim's hideaway after Jim's marriage. The guilt Bryan suffered over being the third occupant of their two-seater still brought bile up into his throat.

To Bryan's mind, Jim's father had coerced him into that loveless marriage with Jackie. The senior Mattock had threatened to cut Jim out of his will and take away any and all financial support if Jim didn't marry and produce an heir.

Jim needed that money because he was starting an innovative technology company. Bryan had first helped him by giving Jim an inheritance Bryan received from his grandmother. It was only a few thousand dollars, but it helped Jim immensely with the startup. Still, Jim needed his father's money to really make it work.

It was a dismal story right out of a melodramatic soap opera. But it was too true. The elder Mattock's were wealthy, and Jim believed his father's threats. Mr. Mattock was so evilly manipulative that it still chilled Bryan to the bone.

Jackie had tried so hard to be a good wife to Jim. She had no way of knowing that her whole marriage was a fraud, a terrible lie that now saddened Bryan every time he thought about it.

Bryan had hated every moment of the secret life he was forced to live in order to be with Jim, who'd introduced Bryan to Jackie as his college frat brother. He shook his head at the memory of the lies he and Jim told Jackie to keep her quiet. He was starting to feel dizzy and sickened at the thoughts.

He and Jim would spend so much time at the condo that Jackie had to know something was going on. Being a bit petty and jealous, Bryan didn't feel guilty at first. It wasn't until Chrystal was born that things started to change between him and Jim.

Jim stayed home with his family longer. He was so proud of his baby girl and his ability to produce such a child. And Chrystal was a beautiful baby. She had a head full of beautiful dark curls and huge sparkling eyes. Jim had suggested the name Chrystal because of those eyes when he saw Jackie and the baby in the hospital.

During those years, Bryan couldn't do anything but pout and bemoan his loneliness, and Jim threatened several times to leave him if he didn't stop.

Jim constantly reminded Bryan that he was only doing what he had to do to appease his crazed father, swearing to Bryan that he didn't love Jackie. Repeatedly saying the marriage would be over soon. Telling Bryan a mountain of lies.

The truth was, Jim really did love Jackie, and it would never be over.

LATER

Bryan's cell phone rang and it startled him out of his dark thoughts. He looked at the display, praying it was Jimmy calling to apologize. Instead, it was Royce.

"Hello." Bryan barely spoke up. His heart was aching him too much. Tears threatened to spill as Royce asked him a couple of questions.

"How you doing Bryan? How you holding up?"

Bryan hesitated for a long moment but finally answered, "I'm trying. That's all I can say for now. Actually, I was thinking of taking a little trip. I need some time away."

"Well, I can say I don't blame you. Dad was pretty cruel to you. I don't understand how he could do the stuff he's doing. He thinks he's the one who's been wronged."

Bryan threw the clothes he had in his hand onto the pile on the bed. He took his time answering Royce, thinking over his choices before he spoke.

"I can't understand him either. To tell you the truth, I feel at a loss as to how to explain any of his actions. I mean, I . . ."

Bryan faltered in his speech. Tears spilled from his eyes onto his jade colored shirt.

"I'm sorry Bryan. If I could change this for you, I certainly would. Have you heard from Dad since we all left Ms. Sylvi's?"

Bryan sat down on his bed and touched the clothes strewn about. He wiped tears from his light-brown eyes and then closed them tightly.

"No, I haven't. I thought maybe he would have called, but he hasn't. Do you think I should go over there? I can get a car service and if nothing else, pick up my car from the garage."

"Yeah that might be a good idea. That way, you can check on him, but won't have to stay if he's still acting up." Royce didn't say more as he waited for Bryan's reply.

"You know he was deep into his whiskey bottle when we left. If he drank all that liquor then his stomach would've rebelled. You know he has gastric problems. He wouldn't admit it, but he really can't manage all that liquor."

"What? No, I didn't know that, I'll give him a call and see what I can find out. I'll talk to you later. Take care."

"Thanks Royce, you take care too." Bryan stayed there on the bed. He thought of the life he'd built with Jim, and anger replaced his sadness.

If he thinks I'm giving up this easily, then he has another think coming. I'm going over there. It's my home too, and I'm not leaving until I get what I need.

Bryan jumped up from the bed and slipped his feet into some sandals from the closet.

"No Jim, I'm not giving up this easily. You're mine, and I'm going to fight for what we have. Whether you like it or not. I'm not going to let you push me out. Not now, not ever."

CHAPTER 4

Jackie Mattock sat on the side of the bed in her mother's house and ran her blue manicured nails absently through her curly, kinky hair. She'd had one of the worst mornings in the history of mornings. Nothing came close except the Saturday morning when she awoke hungover and miserable on the day of her son's wedding.

It was still unreal to her how much she had drunk in her dark emotional state the night before Royce's wedding. She was still reliving a past that was best dead and buried. But as it turned out, it would never be laid to rest.

A good solid tumbler of gin would help, she thought. It was only a little past one in the afternoon, too early to be sloshed.

But she really didn't give a damn at this point. She had a lot of bad memories to try to forget. It appeared she was turning into an alcoholic because of Jimmy.

Had it only been a couple of weeks since the wedding? It was hard to believe all hell had broken loose in such a brief period of time. And apparently, it would never end. It was exhausting to continue to plead her innocence.

Yes, she made some mistakes. Who hadn't, but to constantly be reminded of it and have to explain it, over and over, was too much.

Just looking at her children would never let her forget the things she had done for so-called love. Yet, if she hadn't done those things, there would be no daughter, son, or grandchildren.

She and her sister, Nancy, were still at Ms. Sylvi's house after babysitting Jackie's grandchildren the night before. Chrystal and Tyler were out in the kitchen with Ms. Sylvi and Jackie thought she heard Nancy in the bathroom down the hall.

Jackie's fingers carelessly picked at the colorful hand-made quilt on the bed as her mind mulled over the terrible secrets Chrystal had divulged.

Imagine, Jackie's ex, Jimmy Mattock, was so angry with her and Royce's biological father, Eric Henderson, that he tried to put a hit on them.

It was absolutely absurd. Only Jimmy would be so overly dramatic that he would even contemplate such things as thugs, hit men and murder.

Why in God's name did he even care after more than twenty-five years and an ugly divorce, especially when she practically let him and Bryan walk away unscathed? She had let them off the hook after much soul-searching.

But now, after what he had tried to do to her, she realized she had given her ex-husband too much of a reprieve. Jimmy Mattock deserved some serious retribution for all the hell he'd put them through.

Jackie couldn't help it, but her mind returned to that horrific day when life as she knew it went straight to hell.

She'd come home sick and needing rest, but the sight that met her eyes would forever burn like hell fire into her brain. She had walked slowly up the grand staircase in the old Victorian. Hearing mumbling from her bedroom, she'd slowly pushed wide the slightly open door.

After that day, Bryan's words would play on a loop through her thoughts.

"Oh, my God, Jackie! What are you doing here?"

Bryan ran into the suite's bathroom crying all the way. While Jimmy calmly, much too calmly, had rolled over and looked at her.

"I suppose you want an explanation," Jimmy had said.

In that moment, Jackie couldn't even think straight. Her tears fell like a black monsoon. It wasn't that she was so surprised. No, she was absolutely furious they had dared to do their nasty business in her very home.

She had picked up the wooden statute Bryan bought for them as a wedding gift, held it loosely in her hand, and thought of all the ways she could beat both Jimmy and Bryan to death with it.

The idea almost made her smile, but instead she spoke softly so Jimmy had to sit up to hear her. "You're just a sorry-ass, worthless, piece of common shit. Right here in my own damn bed. And to think I gave you everything I had as a woman."

Jackie had trembled violently, rolling the ugly statue around and around in her hands. "I had babies for you. I put my career on the back burner for you, and I put up with your stupid family and friends for you, you down-low piece of slime. You bring your lover—your frat brother, you said—you bring him into my home and fuck him in my bed! I gave you everything I had to give as your wife, and this is how you repay me?"

Jimmy glared at her as he slowly swung his legs off the side of the bed. He gave Jackie a disgusted look. "Jackie," he said, "put that statute back on the dresser, and sit your ass down right now."

Without realizing it, Jackie moved even closer to the bed. "I tried to change myself into whatever you told me to be because I loved you."

Her eyes were so blinded with scalding, red-hot tears she didn't realize Jimmy had gotten up and was wrapping the sheet around him until he pulled the piece of wood out of her hands.

"Are you finished with your moaning and groaning?" Jimmy took Bryan's gift and tenderly placed it on the dresser. He then casually sat down in the armchair beside the bed as if he wasn't almost nude. "If so, maybe I can get a word in."

Jackie took a few steps back and shook her head. "You must believe I'm the craziest woman in the world if you think I want to listen to anything you got to say. If I had a gun right now, I'd blow your shitty balls right off."

Jackie was so angry all she could do was wheeze and shake. She hugged her arms around herself and let her ashen tears fall.

Jimmy then told her of his plans for her--how he had used her as a front to look like an upstanding family man in a socially acceptable marriage, how he had never loved her, how he had always been with Bryan.

She had stared at Jimmy as if seeing him for the first time. Were her ears functioning? She couldn't have heard him correctly. "What the hell did you just say?" she finally managed to stammer out, as she wiped snot and tears off her face.

"I said—and listen carefully this time—if I'd known you would be this much trouble, I would have left your ass in that conference room years ago. I've tried my damn best to make you into the woman I needed. You were intelligent, not ugly, seemed to have your head on straight."

Jackie looked at Jimmy unbelievably. This couldn't be the man she married and thought she loved. To have planned exactly how he would use her was the act of a devil. And use her was exactly what he'd done since the beginning.

Jimmy had never been the romantic type, spouting pretty poetry, but this person sitting here was so cold and calculating that he could look her in the eyes and say things he knew would destroy her. He was sitting there, bluntly telling her this bullshit. What kind of hellish maniac had she lain down with?

"Did you plan this whole thing, to let me catch you like this? Was I the biggest fool, that stupid, oh my God . . ."

She could barely get the words out clearly before she was left completely speechless. She was dead from the top of her head to the tips of her toes. It was as if someone had hammered a huge nail into the center of her body, her very heart, and let all her scarlet lifeblood drain out. At that moment she knew the devil was real, and she had married him and now she resided in hell.

49

Jimmy made a sound half way between a laugh and a snort. "Don't be ridiculous. I didn't plan this, and I have grown to care for you all in my own way. I'm not the monster you're trying so fucking hard to paint. Bryan and I have been together since college. He knows me like you never could."

The fact that Jimmy was gay, she understood. Well, sort of. She had suspected for some time. Even that he and Bryan were involved didn't completely surprise her because they were just too damn close to only be frat brothers.

But to use her in this way, as he had, and for so long, with no regard for her as a human being, that shredded her soul to ribbons. She was just another tool to him, a disposable object to be used and discarded.

Jackie suddenly thought about Eric, the love she had given up all because she thought Jimmy loved and needed her. She had thrown away the only good man in her life, and for what? A lying, manipulative, gay bastard!

She wanted to hurt Jimmy so badly. She needed to somehow make him pay for all the years she had wasted trying to make this marriage work.

"Jackie, sit down, and let's discuss this. The kids will be home soon from school, and I don't want them to find us all like this." Jimmy looked nervously towards the bathroom, spreading his hands out to encompass them all.

"What the hell do you care?" she threw the words back over her shoulder. "Remember I'm just a means to an end. I'm too damn stubborn to control. Too selfish to just do what I'm told and ignore all this shit. I couldn't see what was right in front of my own damn face."

The pain of that day still lingered, but now Jackie sat in her mother's house and finally had to admit that she had also done wrong. She'd dumped all her anger at Jimmy on Bryan's back, blaming him for Jimmy's lack of human kindness, love, and compassion towards her.

I shouldn't blame Bryan though, she thought. *He's a victim too of Jimmy's cruelty. How could I not have seen the real man. It was so obvious,* Jackie harrumphed.

I guess it doesn't matter now. What's done is done. If I could undo all the damage that he's caused,

I gladly would. But that was wishful thinking that led to nowhere.

Jackie got up from the bed and went to the window. She looked out at the backyard where the roses were blooming bright, lovely colors. Even under a gray cloudy sky, the yellows, reds, and oranges were a pleasure to look at.

Her mother groomed the bushes to perfection. They were fed and watered just the right amount of nutrients, resulting in gigantic blooms of spectacular color. Jackie had started gardening to help her soul heal after the nasty divorce, but to this day. her roses didn't compare to her mother's.

Jackie pictured the chapel were Royce and his bride Jessica were married. It had been decorated with blush rosebuds and full-blooming roses. The chapel was beautiful and smelled heavenly, but Jimmy had shown up dragging a tired looking Bryan with him.

She'd had no idea he'd been invited. It seemed Royce had managed to surprise her again. She'd thought she'd held her own in the confrontation between her and Jimmy. Jackie had made it plain she hadn't needed him or Bryant at her son's wedding.

But the scene that unfolded after the nuptials had been horrific. She thought back to the disastrous wedding reception where she'd fainted and come to with Eric and Jimmy standing over her.

At that time she hadn't seen or spoken to Eric in over ten years. It was a shock to see the love still in his eyes as he looked at her. After so many years of guilt and shame at what she had let herself become, it appeared he still cared for her.

And then the tell-all that sparked so much hatred occurred here, in this same house she grew up in. Although now it had been added on so many times by her late father, it felt and looked like a maze. He had said he wanted room enough for all his children and grandchildren to stay if they ever needed a place. He had loved them all so much.

Although she missed him with all her heart, she was glad her father wasn't here to see how far she had fallen. There wasn't a better man than her father, Buddy Stinson.

The accident that took his life was still too fresh, too difficult to process for everyone, especially her mother. Two long years had passed, but it still seemed like yesterday when he was taken from them.

Jackie was glad, in a way, that her father hadn't been there to see the spectacle. She just knew her mother and sister must think she was all kinds of sluts after that Saturday afternoon. She thought of herself that way also. How it must have looked to them to hear of her promiscuity with a man not her husband.

They'd heard how she believed Eric was the father of both Chrystal and Royce, and that she had been fornicating with him for years while she was married to Jimmy.

It still brought tears to her eyes to confess her sins to her mother, even though Jackie was well pass the age of consent when her long affair with Eric happened.

Here she stood, almost fifty years old, and she was still just as ashamed as a naive teenager caught in the act on prom night.

Jackie and Eric reconciled even though Eric found out he was only Royce's biological father and not Chrystal's. The afternoon had seemed interminable, but in the end healing had occurred.

She and Eric were now back together, something she hadn't imagined possible, but Jimmy was still lurking in the alley, trying to destroy any happiness they could find. She had thought he was through with her and Eric, even though she knew Jimmy had been beyond angry. But to go this far was unbelievable.

Chrystal and Tyler had shared such bizarre news this morning that Jackie had felt like she was watching a bad made-for-TV movie. She'd called Eric when Chrystal finished telling everyone her story. She needed to share this with him. It had sounded so crazy that she felt foolish telling it, but it was all true, too true. He needed to know the depths Jimmy's hateful behavior could reach. He needed to be warned.

It was all painful, though nothing compared to the hurt of finding out Chrystal and Royce had reconciled with their father behind her back. That's when Jimmy had done his paternity tests and said only Chrystal was his.

Their meetings with Jimmy had gone on for years, unbeknownst to her. It made her feel stupid and betrayed for being so unaware of what was going on in her own home with her own children.

Some things could never be undone or forgotten; only time, she prayed, could heal the hurt she felt at their betrayal.

After she'd called Eric and told him everything, he'd immediately said he would be flying in later that day. She needed his comforting touch badly. Eric was her one calming haven in a sea of turbulent disorder.

Now she needed to talk with Chrystal. She wasn't if the story Chrystal told was the whole truth. She believed what her daughter said, but was that really all there was to it? It felt like something was missing. Some parts of Chrystal's story didn't hold up to scrutiny, especially now that so much more had become known.

Why was Chrystal so involved with Smoke and Duck? Chrystal hung with her cousin Nikki, but it seemed to Jackie that Nikki was running the show. It was strange because wasn't normally the type to let Nikki lead her around like that.

Then again, what did she know. She, as a mother, hadn't even noticed Chrystal was pregnant with any of her three children until she was told, let alone all the trouble she was in with Oro's father. Chrystal never confided in her own mother.

Again, so much of this ugliness landed squarely on Jackie's own shoulders. Her lack of parental guidance, her lack of trust and understanding, and lastly but most importantly, her lack of the love she should have shown her only daughter.

Jackie said she forgave Chrystal and understood, but did she really? She had hugged Chrystal to her and said, "Don't cry baby. You didn't intentionally do this. Your father has always been a manipulator. He's the evilest bastard in the world. It's in his DNA, apparently. You're just as much a victim as the rest of us."

Chrystal had cried on her shoulder and continued to beg for forgiveness.

"Mama, I'm so sorry. What can I do to make it up to you? Daddy is . . . I don't know, I just don't know."

"Look, baby, you did what any young girl or woman would have. You love your father and look up to him. Don't ever blame yourself for loving someone. It's just that he has so much hate in his heart. So much anger. It's scary what that can do to a person. Don't let his hate rule your life. Don't turn into an evil person because of him. You can do better than that."

Now Jackie moved silently to the door, still feeling sorry for herself. She said the words to Chrystal about not hating, but she was full of hatred for Jimmy. She knew in her heart that she could never forgive him and truthfully she didn't want to.

Just as she was entering the hallway, her sister Nancy, exited the bathroom.

"How you feeling little sister?" Nancy reached out to hug Jackie to her side.

Jackie laid her head on Nancy's shoulder for a quick moment and said, "I'm doing. Just going through the motions really. I was just going to check on Mama and the grands. Hey, I know how I feel about this latest Jimmy mess, but what about you?"

Nancy moved to lead Jackie down the hallway and answered, "Well, I'm still kinda in shock. You know I have never liked Jimmy, but God, that man is despicable. He not only treated you like crap, but the guy he's supposed to care about he treats like shit too."

They made their way to the living room and stopped. Jackie sat down in a rocking chair and leaned back for a moment. Nancy stood and looked uncertainly at Jackie.

"Yeah, you're right," Jackie said. "Jimmy is a piece of work. Nobody knows better than me that his mind is eaten through with maggots. But like you, I thought he really cared about Bryan. To kick him out and be this stubborn about all this . . . I just don't know. He's crazy, and he's making the rest of us crazy too."

Jackie wiped her eyes with the back of her hand. She slowly rocked and hummed. Finally, she looked sadly at Nancy.

"I feel like this is all my fault. If I hadn't been so needy, with so little self-worth, I would have seen the real person behind the slick smile and Italian suits. I should have been strong enough to take what I wanted, not worry about how my life looked to other people. I should have had more compassion for my own daughter. I should have been a real mother to Chrystal and Royce. The list goes on and on. I feel like I can never make it up to Chrystal, to Royce, to myself."

Nancy crossed her arms under her breasts and scoffed. "Are you finished with the pity party? Just how long are you going to keep beating yourself up? Girl, if you had all this power to see into the future and do all this stuff, then you should have been playing the lottery. We could all be rich now."

Jackie laughed at Nancy's words. "You know, you're always right about everything, but I just want happiness for everybody. I don't want to spend my life looking over my shoulder, waiting for crazy Jimmy to do something else foul. I feel like an idiot for letting all this get out of control."

"Look, I'm going to say this one last time. Stop with the boo-hooing, woe-is-me party. Pull up them big-girl panties and put some steel in your backbone. I know our mother and father didn't raise no quitter. You got a man who loves you. You got two children who adore you. You have a mother who would give her all just to see you smile, and you got a big sister who's tired of hearing your put-downs. You got a whole lot going for you, and you better stop this shit about your self-worth ain't nothing."

"Yeah, you're right. And do you know what?"

"What my wonderful little sister?" Nancy gave Jackie a puzzled look waiting to hear what she would say now.

"I just pulled up my very tight, big-girl panties, and I'm ready to get on with my life. If nothing else, all this has taught me to take back my life before some other fool starts taking over."

Nancy laughed aloud and gave Jackie two thumbs up. "You are exactly right and you better start right now, before those panties get stuck in that fat booty."

Jackie laughed out loud as she grabbed Nancy's hands in her hands. "And you know what else? I am not going to take Jimmy's words for the truth. He said only Royce was Eric's son. I bet that's a big lie too. I'm going to get my own DNA tests done." Jackie stood up straighter with her announcement.

"You know Eric will be here this afternoon. We can get him and Chrystal tested as soon as he gets here. There's more to Jimmy's crazy anger at me and Eric than he's admitting. I should have thought of this before. I shouldn't have just taken his word. Jimmy Mattock is the vilest man I know and he will say and do anything to hurt me."

Jackie released Nancy's hands and gave her a serious look. "Yeah, that's what I'm going to do. I'll bet my last money that Chrystal is Eric's child too."

"I'll take some of that action because I believe you're absolutely correct, lil' sis. Yep, I think you've finally hit the nail over Jimmy's big, evil head."

CHAPTER 5

Royce looked down at his cellphone as it continued to ring. This was the third time he dialed his father's number. But this time, he decided to leave a message.

"Hi Dad. It's me, Royce. I was just checking on you. I know last night was pretty awful, but it's a new day, and I hope things are better. Give me a call back. We're worried about you. Okay, talk to you later."

Royce shook his head at the foolishness that had gone on with his father, Chrystal, and Bryan. Their story was so wild that he had no choice but to believe it.

And to think his father Jimmy, had conspired to hurt his mother. No matter how you looked at it, the evidence was clear and damaging. James "Jimmy" Mattock was one sick, psychotic person.

"Hey bae, what's on your mind? Jessica asked. And don't tell me 'nothing' because you're rubbing your hair over and over. You know that's your tell right." Jessica took the dish towel she had been holding and threw it back on the kitchen counter. She had just finished washing dishes and wiping down the countertops when she heard Royce talking on his cell.

"You know what, that was a stupid question," she said. "Of course, all kinds of things are running through your mind right now. I know how overwhelmed everyone is feeling, but I know it will get better." Jessica picked up the towel, folded it and put it away.

"Come here my new wife. So you think you know my tells, huh?"

"Yes I do," said Jessica as she moved into the small living to join her husband. "I know that one and some others too, but I'm not going to give them all away." Jessica tried to smile at Royce, but the air was thick with the worry coming off him.

Royce pulled Jessica to him and hugged her tight. "You're right as always. I guess I was trying not to bother you with all the details but you're my wife now, and there's no way I want our marriage to start out with secrets and miscommunication. There's been so much of that with my family already."

"Yeah, but it's not just your family. Everybody's family has stuff going on. People are just people. We all make mistakes, and believe me, my family has skeletons in their closets too. So, spill it. After this morning's revelations, I don't think anything else will surprise me."

"Well, I talked to Bryan a little while ago. He's at his condo and packing to go away. He's so torn up about Dad's behavior. I know he feels shattered. And I don't blame him. But he told me he hadn't heard from Dad, and he's worried about him. Apparently, Dad has really bad stomach problems and can't take all the alcohol he was drinking."

"Oh wow! Did you know about that? I mean drinking too much can be deadly for someone with stomach problems. My uncle passed away from an ulcerated and bleeding stomach. But he was a chronic alcoholic." Jessica rubbed Royce's arm as he continued to hold her.

"No, I didn't know about Dad. You know how secretive he is, but anyway, I told Bryan I would call him and check it out. I called twice with no answer, and then I left him a message. Of course, he hasn't called back. But I get the feeling Bryan isn't finished with Dad yet. I bet he goes over there. Besides, it's his home too, and he has every right to go to his home. I just hope Dad has sobered up and is ready to do the right thing. If not, I know all hell's gonna break loose again."

"Poor Bryan. I don't know how he puts up with the things your dad does. He really loves him." Jessica moved out of Royce's arms and sat on the sofa.

"You got to have a lot of patience and kindness in your heart to forgive the stuff your dad said to him. I don't think I could be that forgiving."

Royce followed Jessica over to the sofa and sat with her. "So you're telling me you wouldn't forgive me for a little white lie?"

"I hardly think what your dad has done qualifies as a little white lie. The mess he's made with his relationships with Chrystal and Bryan, not to mention your mother, tops the list of monstrous red lies. But you my husband, I would forgive you anything. Mainly because I know you would never do anything to hurt me. I'm certain of your love for me, just as I know you are certain of mine."

Royce reached for Jessica's hand and held it between his palms. As he rubbed her hand, he said, "Yes my lovely. I would rather die than hurt you in any way. And I promise if I ever do anything to hurt you, you have the right to kick my sorry ass to the curb and get you another man."

Jessica laughed at the serious look Royce was giving her and said, "You got a bet." But deep down, she knew the mess with Royce's family wasn't over. In fact she believed this was just the start of more trouble to come.

"Hey, how about something less serious? You know the gift your father and Bryan gave us for this townhome makeover?"

"Sure, what about it?" Royce stood and moved to the small kitchen, where he rummaged around in the refrigerator.

Jessica followed. "I know you're not looking for more food. You just finished that huge deli sandwich with chips and everything."

"Look Bae, I am still growing. I need more than just a sandwich sometimes. Besides, that was a half hour ago. I got to keep my stamina up so I can pleasure you." Royce smirked and looked to Jessica for confirmation.

Jessica laughed at the look on Royce's face. "You know what? You're just full of yourself."

"Don't come to me when your stomach is sticking out like a pregnant woman. I'm just gonna laugh and laugh. Pleasuring me . . . right. Like for real?"

"Okay, okay. I was just joking. Anyway, what about the townhouse redo?"

Royce finally pulled a soda out of the refrigerator and leaned against the countertop.

"Well, I was thinking about going ahead and scheduling a time for the people to come out and meet with us. We might as well get started on that. But things are so estranged between Bryan and your father, I just don't know. What do you think?"

"I think we need to schedule a time and get started. And yes, things are funky with Bryan and Dad, but that's their problem for the most part. There's nothing we can do about that anyway."

"I know, but I feel so bad about their break up. It just hurts me to think how happy they were to give us the gift and now things are just so crazy."

"Yeah, I know. You feel too much, my beautiful wife. But anyway, I was thinking about the gift from my grandparents also. Twenty-five thousand dollars is a lot of money, and we need to decide what we want to do with that too." Royce tenderly kissed Jessica's forehead and released her.

"It's great to see that balance in the bank, but we need to better manage it and make it work for us. I don't know if we'll ever see that kind of money from them again, what with me being Eric's biological son."

"You, my darling husband are correct, as usual, and since you live only for pleasuring me, I suggest you get started with the loving. I think we both could use that. Am I right?"

Royce pulled Jessica to him and said, "Sho you right bae, sho you right."

CHAPTER 6

It was 2:30 in the afternoon on what had turned out to be a gray June day. Bryan could feel the pressure of an impending thunderstorm. He sat in the back seat of the service's car and entered a tip on the app as they pulled up to the house he shared with Jim. He thanked the driver before he stepped out.

Bryan cautiously looked to the front doors of his home. They were beautiful with their stately, elegantly carved glass in a bronze frame. His heart beat frantically in his chest, and his palms were sweating buckets as he stared at his and Jim's home.

He and Jim had moved years ago from the renovated Victorian in Midtown. Bryan had loved that house, but after the disastrous encounter he, Jim, and Jackie had there, the place felt poisoned with misery and unfaithfulness.

Bryan used to love to walk through the house, marveling at the intricately carved woodwork on the grand staircase. It spoke to him in a way the new house never could. It eased his soul and reminded him of the grand old houses of New Orleans.

But they'd sold the renovated Victorian at a big profit and had taken only personal items—clothes and an extensive art collection—and started over in this brand-new house.

Jim had left all the furniture in the old house, including the king-size Regency bed that had been Jim's greatest joy. Bryan never wanted to see that damn bed again after the horrible day Jackie had caught them both in it together.

To this day, he couldn't get that encounter out of his head. Jackie had looked at him with such fury in her eyes. Although he couldn't blame her for her emotions, it still hurt him and stirred up guilt every time he saw her.

He'd asked Jim, over and over, if he'd planned to let Jackie catch them in the act, and each time, Jim had played it off as if the dramatic situation wasn't much of anything to worry about.

They had furnished the new house with every convenience and toy on the market, even going as far as hiring a *feng shui* consultant, which Bryan had to have, that and other eccentricities

They had poured every dream wish into the new house, but it still felt wrong, empty somehow, devoid of life, love, and happiness.

Now Bryan took three huge breaths and slowly walked the manicured pathway to the front door. Everything outside the house looked the same as when he walked away. But in his heart he knew exterior looks could be deceiving.

I feel like a fool doing this, he thought. *I wonder what Jim's gonna say when I walk in.*

He hesitated, thinking of getting back in the car as the driver turned down the circular driveway and drove away. Bryan searched his mind for some snappy comeback to what he imagined Jim might say to him.

Jim would likely say: "Well, look what the cat dragged in." To which Bryan would reply, "At least I don't look like a cat who's been drowned in whiskey." *Yeah that's pretty good. Just keep it mild.*

Don't go ballistic about anything negative he might say.

Bryan reached into his shorts pocket and took out his key. He rubbed his empty, sweaty hand up and down his shorts and then switched to his other hand and did the same. He was nervous, and he was scared of what he might find when he opened the door to his own house.

The walk seemed to end too quickly and before he knew it he was standing at the elaborate double doors. *Well, here goes nothing as Jim loves to say.*

Bryan slowly turned his key in the lock, but he was surprised to find the door wasn't locked as it should have been. Jim always checked and double-checked the locks before going to bed. He could never rest if he hadn't secured the doors and set the alarm. Already, Bryan was wondering what was going on.

"Jim! Jim, it's me!" Bryan yelled out as he came into the foyer. He figured he might as well give Jim a little warning so he wouldn't attack as if Bryan were an intruder.

Silence.

Bryan moved further into their home. He didn't hear Jim at all. He went into the kitchen. Everything looked normal there, but no sign of Jim. He went through the spacious mudroom, then over to the door that led to the garage.

Still sitting in their usual spots were both his sporty white Range Rover and Jim's black Jaguar. The third car bay held Jim's classic red Corvette that he loved so well. *Well, he hasn't gone anywhere, unless he used a car service,* Bryant thought. *Okay, he must be in the family room, still pouting.*

Bryan hesitantly walked down the hallway to the family room. The tension he was feeling was so tight, he thought his head might burst.

The door to the room was slightly open. As he pushed it and peered into the room, he almost lost the contents of his stomach. There was his Jim, lying on the Burmese carpet with bloody vomit seeping from his mouth.

Bryan stood still for a long moment. He rubbed his eyes as if he were seeing something unbelievable. And for him, seeing Jim on the floor was unbelievable.

As if he'd been forcefully propelled forward by some unseen force, Bryan stumbled into the room and dropped to his knees beside Jim.

"Oh my God! Jim! Jim, do you hear me?"

He felt for a pulse at Jim's neck and was relieved to find one. Bryan rolled Jim slowly to his side and used his shirt bottom to wipe the mess on Jim's mouth. Tears steadily fell from Bryan's eyes and dripped down his cheeks.

Jim groaned as Bryan was caring for him. He made some unintelligible sounds and Bryan bent his head lower to hear.

"Jim, what have you done to yourself? You know you shouldn't drink like this. This is just suicide."

Jim made another sound and Bryan bent even lower to hear.

"What did you say? Are you all right?"

"What, what in the hell are you doing here? How dare you!" Jim hissed the words from a foul-smelling mouth.

Bryan jerked back from Jim's cruelty. He was stunned. Here Jim lay, where he couldn't even get his sorry ass up from the floor, blood, and vomit oozing from his mouth, and he was still being the same arrogant asshole he'd been the day before.

"Get, get out. Get out!" Jim made a move away from Bryan's hand, shaking off his husband's touch. He rolled to his back again and tried to sit up.

Bryan was so shocked, he sat back on his heels and stared disbelievingly at the efforts Jim was making not to touch him. *What a fool! He has to be the evilest man in the world. He's lying here with empty whiskey bottles all over the place, and he's denying the obvious. Oh Lord, why do I even care anymore?*

"You need help, you selfish asshole. I'm calling 9-1-1." Bryan pulled his cell phone from his pocket and started dialing.

"Don't! I'm all right. I don't want your help." Jim managed to move into a sitting position on the floor as he growled at Bryan to stop.

"9-1-1, I have a medical emergency at my home."

"What 's the address sir."

"Ah, the address is 4972 Olde Rockaway."

"Who's in distress?"

"He's a fifty-five year old male and has stomach problems. I think it's alcohol poisoning."

"Is he alert?"

"Yes. He's somewhat alert and sitting on the floor, but there's blood and vomit coming from his mouth."

"We have an ambulance in route. Are you able to remain with the patient."

"Yes, thank you."

Bryan gave Jim a hard look as he clicked off the cell. Focused on the emergency, Bryan had calmed significantly from his initial reaction to Jim's harsh words, but Jim continued to harass him with a negative shaking of his head.

"I. Don't. Want. You. Here." He could barely get the words out. He burped between most of them, and spittle flew from his mouth as he finished.

Bryan sat quietly staring at Jim and wondering who this man really was until sirens could be heard in the distance.

"I don't care anymore what you want," Bryan told him. "I've wasted too much time on what you want. You're selfish and mean, the worst combination one can imagine. But I'm going to do all that I can to help you. You don't deserve it, but I can't let you hurt yourself like this."

They persisted in giving each other hateful looks. Neither said another word. Soon the sirens were right outside the house, and Bryan stood and moved to leave the room. As he made it to the doorway, Jim called out.

"I'll never forgive you for this." With the extra effort of those words, he fell back to the floor.

Bryan shook his head and replied, "Yes, I'm sure you won't. But that's nothing new."

NORTHCENTRAL HOSPITAL

Bryan paced back and forth in the hospital's waiting room. He'd followed the ambulance to Northcentral Hospital and it had been a hellish trip. Fortunately, it wasn't a long drive, but traffic was heavy, and he had trouble keeping up with the ambulance driver's erratic maneuvers through the vehicles.

Thirty minutes had elapsed since he stepped through the hospital doors, but his heart was still racing with adrenaline as if he'd sprinted from his house to the hospital.

Bryan called Royce, and he and Jessica were on their way. Now, he hesitated as he placed a call to Chrystal. He knew how angry she had been, and rightly so, but he felt she needed to know.

"Hello Chrystal baby. I've got some bad news to relay." Bryan looked around the nearly empty waiting room and was glad so few people would hear his side of this telling.

"Hi Bryan. If it's anything to do with Daddy, I don't want to hear about it."

Bryan cringed at Chrystal's words, but he continued anyway. "I'm sorry baby, but your father is in the hospital. We're at Northcentral, and I really do think you need to come."

Bryan could imagine Chrystal rolling her eyes at this statement. There was silence for too long, but finally Chrystal answered.

"What's wrong with him? Have his evil deeds finally caught up to him?"

Bryan heard the scorn in Chrystal's voice and it made him so very sad. "No, Chrystal. Please don't be that way. Your father has an abdominal ulcer, and it's pretty serious. Especially since it seems he drank multiple bottles of whiskey last night."

"That's his fault Bryan. He told me he was grown and could do what he wants. Why should I come to see him just because his stomach hurts? I really am through with him and his games."

Bryan almost shouted into the phone; he was so frustrated. But he really couldn't blame Chrystal for her non-concern. Jim had treated her horrendously, and he deserved her disdain. But Bryan knew he needed to try anyway.

"Listen baby. I went home and found your father on the floor of the family room. He was barely conscious and was bleeding from the mouth and couldn't even get up. I called 9-1-1 and they rushed him here. He's been taken to surgery. I wouldn't have called if it wasn't serious."

"Well thanks for telling me, but I think I'm gonna sit this one out. You can keep me updated, but I'm not coming. I'm sorry for you Bryan, because I know how much you love Daddy, but he killed something inside me when he treated me like he did. I'm a grown-ass woman, and he talked to me like I was a stupid little girl. And he disrespected

Tyler so badly. Not to mention what he planned to do to Mama and Eric. There's no forgiveness coming from me for his doing that shit."

"I know, I know, and I'm sorry baby. I'm so sorry. Maybe one day it won't hurt so much and you can find a way to live with him."

Bryan turned into a corner of the room as he lowered his voice. "You're right about all of his crimes, and I'm not even sure why I still care. But anyway . . ."

"See, you still love him, but me, I'm not so convinced he's worth the effort right now. Like I said you keep me updated, and I'll let mama and the rest know."

Bryan dropped his head and replied slowly, "Okay, honey. I'll talk to you later. Bye."

"Bye, Bryan. Take care."

Bryan clicked off his phone. He looked behind him to see if he was still pretty much alone. There were two other people in the large waiting room. They seemed to be minding their own business.

He turned from the wall so slowly that he wondered to himself if some horrible ailment had suddenly come upon him. He reached blindly for the closest chair and sat heavily in it. *Oh, my Lord. I feel terrible.*

Sweat was rolling down Bryan's face and wetting his shirt. He picked up a magazine that was several years old and fanned himself. His breathing seemed to have stuck in his chest. The usual in and out didn't seem to be working anymore.

Bryan took shallow breaths and tried to calm himself. He realized Chrystal's refusal to come to the hospital was making him physically sick. He looked up from the old gardening magazine to find the eyes of the other people in the room looking at him uncertainly.

"Sir, are you okay?" A young man was looking intently at Bryan while he hugged a small child to his side.

Bryan continued to fan himself, but finally answered. "Yes, thank you. I just got more sad news. That's all. Today has been pretty rough."

"Do I need to call the doctor for you? You look way too pale." Bryan noticed the young man hugged the child closer to his side, as if whatever Bryan was dealing with was contagious.

"No, no, I'm okay. Thank you for your concern. I just need to make another call. Thanks."

Bryan stood again on wobbly legs and headed to a corner as far away from the young man and the child as possible. He really was not feeling well, but he knew who he needed to call next.

"Hello, Mr. Mattock. This is Bryan Denveue. Jim's . . ." Bryan hesitated for a long moment. *This is so stupid,* he thought. *I don't even know what to call myself when I'm talking to this man.*

"Hello Bryan, how are you and James?"

"Well sir, I'm afraid I have some bad news for you and your wife."

The Mattock's were due to fly home to Denver sometime tonight after being in Alpharetta for the past few days. They had reconciled somewhat with Jim, Chrystal, and Royce after years of estrangement.

Theirs was an odd family to say the least, but Bryan felt he needed to tell them about their son before they left. He hesitated again, but finally he came out with it.

"Sir, James is in the hospital. He's in surgery as we speak. He has an ulcerated stomach and esophagus. The doctors are working to stop the bleeding and repair the damage done. It's very serious."

"Hold on Bryan, let me get Mrs. Mattock so she can hear." A moment later, James Sr. came back to the phone. "Go ahead. Please repeat what you said for my wife."

Bryan patiently told the Mattock's what had happened. They both wanted to come to the hospital. Even though their flight was to leave around eight, they said they would come as soon as possible.

"Okay Mr. and Mrs. Mattock. I'll be here in the waiting room. Royce and Jessica are also on their way here. I'll let you know if anything changes before then. Goodbye."

Well, that's all I can do for now. Bryan turned back around and scanned the room. It was empty now. Apparently, the young man and child had decided they'd had enough of his erratic ways. He was thankful for the reprieve. He didn't feel like he could say another word to anyone at the moment.

Bryan sat heavily in a chair close to the wall and willed himself to calm down. After a long moment, he felt better and checked his phone. Another half hour had passed since he first came in. He must have actually dozed for a moment. Suddenly exhausted, he hung his head and brought a hand up to his forehead.

Together, the events of last night, this morning, and this afternoon were much more than he could manage. He was so tired. No, he was beyond tired. He was scratching at the very last threads of his sanity, and they were unraveling faster than he could fathom. Time continued to pass, but he had no idea how much.

NORTHCENTRAL HOSPITAL – 5:00PM

Royce and Jessica hurried into the waiting room, and Jessica sat beside Bryan and rubbed his arm.

"Bryan, man, are you okay?" She looked up worriedly at Royce when he greeted a clearly exhausted Bryan.

"I'm so sorry." Bryan rubbed his eyes and sighed deeply. "I didn't mean to worry you guys but I'm afraid I can't take too much more. It's been a hellish couple of weeks. But enough about me."

"That's all right. We're here for you. Let go of some of that heavy load. Royce and I will help you any way we can. Have you heard anything on Mr. Mattock's surgery."

Jessica continued to rub Bryan's arm. She looked from Bryan to Royce, tilting her head towards Bryan.

Royce said, "That's right, Bryan. Don't feel as if you're in this by yourself. We're here to help. Have you reached Chrystal yet?"

Royce sat in the chair on the other side of Jessica and nodded his head to her, signaling that they were in agreement.

When Bryan looked up, tears had pooled in his eyes. "I haven't heard a thing yet. Oh, my Lord! I don't know what to do. I called Chrystal, but she refused to come. She said . . . she said she didn't care, basically. I understand how she feels, but I thought she was more forgiving, more loving. I guess I was wrong again. You Mattock's are hard people to keep on trying to love."

Royce smiled at Jessica and said, "You're right. We can be difficult, but if you really love somebody then it'll be good. Maybe not at first, but eventually we'll grow on you." Royce took Jessica's hand in his and kissed the back of it. He gave her a tender look, and she smiled back in reply.

"Well, right now I feel like 'eventually' is not due for a good many years. I don't know if I have the fortitude to last that long." Bryan shook his head and sat up straighter in the chair.

"By the way, I called your grandparents. They aren't due to leave town until tonight. I filled them in on Jim's condition, and they said they would come as soon as possible. That was a little while ago, so I guess they'll be here soon."

"Mattock family?" A middle-aged doctor walked slowly up to Bryan, Royce, and Jessica. He had a tactful look on his face.

"Yes, I'm his husband, Bryan Denveue." Bryan sprang up from his chair and clasped his hands together.

"Hello, I'm Doctor Floyd. We've finished surgery on Mr. Mattock. For now, he's in critical, but stable condition, but his blood pressure has been fluctuating, and I'm concerned about that. We gave him a pint of blood because of the loss from the hemorrhaging. He's been sedated to keep him from removing his IV and to keep his blood pressure steady."

"Oh no! Doctor Floyd, I'm his daughter-in-law Jessica, and this is his son, Royce, my husband. What do you mean? Is he combative or just in distress?"

The doctor nodded at both Jessica and Royce. "Well, he is agitated. When he came to in the recovery room, he was not in the best of moods. I believe he was saying your name, Mr. Denveue. After we moved him to intensive care, that's when he tried to remove his IV."

"That damn Jim," Bryan said, I should've of known he wouldn't be happy. He didn't want to come to the hospital, Dr. Floyd. I'm the one who found him and called 9-1-1. He didn't want my help, but . . ."

Bryan stopped talking and shrugged. He looked sadly at Royce and Jessica.

"It's all right Bryan. You did the right thing. Dad is just being his usual pigheaded self. Dr. Floyd, can we see my father?" Royce looked questioningly at the doctor.

"Not right now. Like I said we sedated him, so he could settle down. Give us a couple of hours, and then we'll see. I just wanted to update you on his condition."

The doctor turned as James Sr. and MaryBeth came rushing into the waiting room. They both looked distraught.

MaryBeth had tears streaking her pale complexion, but she managed to give everyone a small smile and nod. "Bryan, Royce, Jessica, how are you all? How's James?"

The senior Mattock moved to stand between Bryan and Jessica. He hugged Jessica to his side and reached out a hand to shake Bryan's.

Royce moved to Mrs. Mattock's side and hugged her. "We were just getting the update from Dr. Floyd, Grandmother. Dad's in critical but stable condition, but he's in intensive care. How are you holding up?"

"Yes, Dr. Floyd here told us we will have to wait awhile to see Jim. He's still under sedation. Isn't that correct, doctor?" said Bryan wringing his hands.

The doctor cleared his throat and replied, "Yes, he had a significant amount of internal bleeding due to an ulcerated esophagus and stomach. But the surgery was successful, and you should be able to see him in a few hours. Thanks everyone. I have to get back to my patients, but here's my card. Call me if you have any more questions."

All eyes were on the doctor as he left the room. The room's occupants were quiet and looked around nervously. Royce was the first one to speak up as he hugged his grandmother close.

"Grandfather, really, how are you?"

"I'm sorry to have to be together for this reason, but I can't complain. Your grandmother is the one we need to take care of. She's not in the best of health, and now, with James here in the hospital . . ." James Sr. trailed off and looked to his wife.

"I'm all right James'" MaryBeth said. "I told you nothing will keep me from my son and grandchildren again. I feel so much better just being here, surrounded by my family. By the way, Royce, where's Chrystal?"

Royce stared at Bryan. Bryan returned the stare with a blank look. Jessica cleared her throat to say something, but Royce cut her off.

"She's still at our grandmother's house. You know she is moving in with her, and they were settling a lot of things today. I'm sure she'll be here after they finish with all that." Royce gave Bryan another silent, knowing look.

"Yes, yes, I'm sure she will." Bryan said a silent prayer. *Please, Lord, please let her come. If not for Jim's sake, then for her own.*

CHAPTER 7

Chrystal came back inside her grandmother's house through the kitchen door and settled in the family room. She had paced the family room floor while Bryan told her what was going on with her father. But she couldn't take it all in.

She didn't know what to do at the time, so instead of deciding, she had gone outside to the patio and procrastinated. *This whole situation with Daddy is just plain bull. He can't be that sick. He's too mean and stubborn to be that sick.*

She squirmed on the softly upholstered chair as a new text came in. She took a deep breath and opened the text. It was from Royce, and now she was more conflicted than ever.

"Chrystal, please. Dad is in pretty bad shape and Bryan isn't doing much better. Please come to the hospital."

Jackie came into the room and sat on the sofa opposite Chrystal. "Hi baby, I was looking for you. What's wrong now? What's that look on your face about?"

"Well." Chrystal hesitated a long moment before answering. "I got a call from Bryan a little while ago. He's really upset. And just now Royce texted me about the same thing. Apparently, Daddy drunk himself into the hospital. They're at Northcentral Hospital waiting on Daddy to get out of recovery from surgery."

"What? You've got to be kidding me! I swear that man is too much." Jackie turned towards the door when Nancy came in and asked what was going on.

"Hey, Aunt Nancy." Chrystal tried but failed to muster a smile. "Would you please tell Grandma and Tyler to come here? That way, I can tell you all at the same time."

Chrystal took a thick piece of her hair and twisted it around and around her finger. Jackie gave Nancy a quick shake of her head in frustration.

"Sure. Hold on a minute. I can tell this is going to be another juicy story." Nancy hurriedly returned with Ms. Sylvi and Tyler, who had been talking together in the kitchen.

"Okay, everyone, Bryan called me." Chrystal looked to the ornate clock on the wall and noted the time. "Well, actually quite a while ago now. He said he went to their house and found Daddy passed out on the floor."

"What? Oh my Lord! Why didn't you tell us before now?" Ms. Sylvi dropped heavily into her favorite chair and fanned her face with her hand. She suddenly looked much older than her seventy-six years.

"I'm sorry, Grandma, but I didn't want to believe it myself. And besides, Daddy has been such a piece of work that I kind of thought he deserved to be sick. Anyway, Royce just texted me and said he and Jessica are at the hospital. Daddy's parents are there also. He's out of surgery, but they're keeping him sedated for a while."

Chrystal stood up and started pacing again. She passed in front of Tyler, and he reached out and took her hand in his. He pulled her to him, stopping her frantic movements.

"Don't worry." Tyler hugged Chrystal to his chest and moved her twisted hair behind her ear. "I'm sure your dad will be okay. Like you said before, he's tougher than nails and twice as sharp."

"Chrystal, what are you not telling us? It just feels like something else is going on." Jackie gave Chrystal a knowing look.

Chrystal clung to her fiancé as she scanned the room and took in the expressions of concern from her mother, aunt, and grandmother. She leaned her head on Tyler's shoulder.

"I guess I didn't want to still be treated like a child anymore. So when Bryan asked me to come to the hospital to see Daddy, I told him no. I kinda said I didn't care and wouldn't be coming to see him since he treated us all like trash. I know Bryan was very upset, but at the time, I just didn't care. In fact I still don't care."

Jackie stood up and went to her daughter to hug her even as Chrystal remained in Tyler's embrace.

"Baby, I know how awful this has been for you," Jackie said, "and Tyler also. But Jimmy is your father, and as hard as it is for me to say this, you owe him a certain amount of respect. You should have told us Bryan called. If your father was in that serious condition, then we had a right to know. Do you understand what I'm trying to say?"

Chrystal lowered her head. "I hear you, Mama, but I believe you have to earn your respect, and Daddy has killed something inside me. I just don't feel he can be trusted. He's passed the point of no return with me. I think he's getting what he deserves. We didn't poison him with alcohol. He drank that whiskey all by himself because he wanted to. In fact, Bryan begged him to stop drinking, but he wouldn't. He must've known he had stomach problems. So, as they say, karma is a real bitch."

Everyone in the room looked at each other, and to a person, they all silently agreed with Chrystal's assessment.

"So, does this mean the plans for our girls cruise is off?" Nancy looked at Jackie with a slight smile on her face. "I mean there's no way crazy-ass

Jimmy and depressed Bryan can keep the kids now while we go and celebrate my retirement. Can they?"

Jackie looked to their mother, and Ms. Sylvi, in turn, looked at Chrystal. Chrystal gave them all a noncommittal hunch of her shoulders.

The only answering sound heard was the excited chatter of Jewell, Oro, and Jade, playing happily in the kitchen.

NORTHCENTRAL HOSPITAL – 7:00PM

Jimmy Mattock awoke to quiet talking. He couldn't remember why it felt as if he was lying in a small bed. He didn't know where he was. He had a strange feeling this was déjà vu, for he remembered waking up earlier, confused and in pain.

He pretended to sleep and listened to the whispering going on around him. He heard several voices. A couple sounded like women, but he couldn't place a face or name with either voice.

He tried to crack an eye to see where he was, but his eyes refused to cooperate. So, much to his dismay, he had to rely on his hearing.

"I can't understand why he did this to himself. Were things that out of control, to the point he would risk his life that way?" a woman whispered.

Jimmy turned his head slightly in the direction he thought the voices were coming from. Still unable to distinguish who or what, he silently fumed

Next he heard the louder but still quiet mumblings of a deeper voice, and to his confused mind it sounded like his father. But that couldn't be right. His father never lowered his voice, no matter who he was talking to.

It couldn't be his mother and father. They'd left his house hours ago. And they certainly wouldn't be in his bedroom, whispering behind his back. Jimmy would never allow his father in his private suite.

Besides, they should be on a plane, heading back to Denver. That much he was sure of. He remembered their visit, and he remembered they were leaving on Saturday night. Unless this wasn't Saturday night.

It occurred to Jimmy that he must be hallucinating. There was no way the voices he heard now would be in the same room together with his tyrant of a father. For now he distinctly heard Bryan who was talking and sobbing. *Should've known Bryan would be crying like a bitch somewhere.*

Was he dead? That must be the reason he couldn't open his eyes. In a rush, it all came back to him. The ridiculous situation with Chrystal and Bryan trying to pin him down and incriminate him flooded his mind.

He remembered drinking whiskey until he passed out. And a hazy recollection of Bryan kneeling beside him on the floor of his family room came back full force.

I must be dead and in hell, he thought. *There's no other reason for this group of people to be together.* He strained even more to hear what was being said about him.

The women's voices became clearer, and he could sort out his mother's voice and Jessica's also. *So where Jessica is, so must Royce be, that traitor of a so-called son.*

99

Jimmy didn't know which was angering him more, his father being near or Royce looking down upon his dead body.

He hated them all, and even in his death, he had no forgiveness of what he considered his family's treacherous betrayal.

"Take it easy Bryan, Dad's going to be fine. Dr. Floyd said he's sedated. Don't worry, he'll pull through."

Yes, that was Royce all right. But he said I'll be fine. And he mentioned a doctor. So I must not be dead, just in the hospital.

Jimmy calmed down knowing he wasn't dead, but in the next moment he heard Bryan's voice, and that started his blood to boil.

Too close to his ear, he heard Bryan whispering.

"Jim, why were you so foolish? You knew better than to drink all that damn whiskey. What were you trying to do? I don't think you care what you do to yourself, and you certainly don't care what happens to the rest of us."

Bryan's words angered him all over again. Not because Bryan was wrong, but because he was so right.

No, I don't give a damn about you or anyone else. You're all deserters. You should all be taken in front of a firing squad. I won't be fooled by your lies ever again.

In his anger, Jim moaned out loud, but his throat was dry and rusty, making it difficult to fully articulate.

He felt tubes running under his nose with little prongs that reached into each nostril, delivering oxygen to his starved brain. Furious with his predicament, he wanted to rip them off.

Every eye in the room swiveled to him as his moans grew louder, and now, not a sound could be heard from any of the occupants.

Bryan bent lower to Jim's face. "Jim, are you awake? Do you hear me?" Bryan hovered over Jim and pulled the covers up around his shoulders.

Mrs. Mattock went to the other side of the bed and held Jimmy's hand in hers. "James? Oh, my goodness! Do you hear me?" She looked back at her husband when Jimmy's eyes started fluttering.

"Oh James, I think he's coming to! Thank you, God."

Jimmy leaned his head towards his mother's hand and fully opened his eyes. He managed to croak out a reply. "Yes, Mother, I hear you. Why . . . why are you here? Where is 'here' anyway?"

"Thank you, Lord," said Bryan from the other side of the bed. "Jim, you're at Northcentral Hospital. You've had surgery to fix the damage from all your outrageous drinking."

"James, we've been so worried about you," said his mother. 'What in the world is going on? Bryan said you drank yourself into this terrible condition. What could possibly be so wrong that you would do this harm to yourself?"

MaryBeth squeezed Jimmy's hand, but he slowly pulled away from her grasp and slid his hand back under the covers. He heard his father cuss under his breath, and Jimmy's heart beat faster.

"Mother, Bryan talks . . . too much and doesn't know what he's talking about. I had a couple, a couple of drinks after a long night. I was just relaxing, that's all."

It hurt his throat to talk, but that wasn't going to stop him from making cutting remarks to everyone listening. Jimmy closed his eyes and didn't say another word.

Everyone in the room, except Jimmy, turned towards the door as Dr. Floyd entered. "Well, I see our patient has come around. How do you feel Mr. Mattock?"

"I feel fine. When can I go home? And who are you, anyway?" Jimmy spoke with his eyes closed.

Under the covers, he moved his hands and felt the dressing that covered the middle of his chest. Next, he moved one hand towards his nose, fingering the tubing there.

But he lied. Jimmy didn't feel fine, in fact, he felt just as bad as, if not worse than, when he'd regained consciousness on the floor of his family room.

Dr. Floyd looked around the room at all the faces that held varying degrees of shock or wariness.

"All right then, but, Mr. Mattock you'll have to stay with us a little while longer. And I'm Dr. Floyd, the emergency room doctor on call. I did a procedure on you to patch the rupture in your stomach. Also, I placed a patch in your esophagus to stop that bleeding. You're a very sick man."

"By his own damn doing, no doubt," murmured James Sr.

Dr. Floyd looked to the senior Mattock and scowled for just a moment.

"We had to give him a few pints of blood to get that blood pressure of his to stabilize. Although now it seems to be rising again from too many discordant factors in this room."

As if emphasizing the doctor's point, the monitors attached to Jimmy beeped louder with an unsteady pattern. Jimmy's heart rate and oxygen levels both moved up and down in opposite directions.

Dr. Floyd moved closer to the monitors, keeping track of Jimmy's vitals by writing something on his tablet. Then he peeled back the covers to check his patient's surgical wound.

Bryan tried to pat Jim's shoulder, but Jimmy pulled away from him. Bryan frowned down at Jim and sighed out loud.

"Dr. Floyd, is there anything we can do about his condition? He seems to be in pain. Or at least,

I'm hoping that's the reason he has such a foul attitude."

"Mr. Denveue, I'm sorry but we have him on pain medication through his IV, but the attitude is all his, I'm afraid. I think he just needs to calm down, and maybe fewer people in his room will help with his blood pressure. I allowed you all in because of this ... particular situation, but now, I really must ask you to leave."

"We understand, Dr. Floyd. We just needed to see with our own eyes how he was doing," said Royce as he pulled Jessica away from the bed and ushered her to the door.

"So, Dr. Floyd, we can return at what time in the morning?" Mrs. Mattock clasped and unclasped her hands, over and over, as she looked from the doctor to her husband, who shook his head in a negative motion.

"Some time after eleven would be good. That way, I can make my rounds and see to our patient here. Is there anything else anyone is confused about before you say goodnight to Mr. Mattock?"

A chorus of "no" filled the room, but Jimmy called out in a ragged voice. "Bryan! When you come back, make sure you bring my phone. I have some calls I need to make, and make sure it's charged up. I do have a multi-million dollar business to run."

Bryan slowed his move towards the door. He turned back to Jim lying in the bed with his eyes closed and said, "Of course Jim. It will be my pleasure to bring back your charged phone. Is there anything else you need, sir?"

As unpleasantly as he could, Jim replied, "That's all. You're dismissed. You all can leave now. I'm tired of this conversation and want to sleep."

After his family and Dr. Floyd filed out of his room, Jimmy lay brooding. In a daze from the drugs and his own anger at his father, he found sleep elusive. The more he thought about his father, the more his blood pressure rose.

He couldn't help but remember growing up with his monster of a father and the torture he'd endured at his hands. Despondently, his mind slipped back to those days, and his hands clinched into fists as he imagined his father's neck in his grip.

CHAPTER 8

Forty Plus Years Ago

James "Jimmy" Mattock Jr. was thirteen when his father divulged his grand plans for him. He wanted no part in his father's foolish schemes, but as in many such families governed by an oppressor, he didn't really have a choice.

His mother, Marybeth and his twelve-year-old sister, Teresa, made up the rest of the Mattock clan that resided in Denver.

The females in the Mattock family were mere shadows in their household. They existed only to do what he ordered. Their opinions and ideas were not something the senior Mattock heeded or even acknowledged. They didn't seem to have a life other than what he allowed them.

He had his ideas of how his family would be, and that was that. After all James Sr. was the only man in the house and definitely the head of the family.

Much like his father, Jimmy put females in a very small compartment in his mind, and when he had used them for his purposes, he tended to ignore them also.

There was such a strong consistency in the males' behavior that no one doubted Jimmy was his father's child.

Marybeth came from a wealthy St. Louis family, originally derived from the creole elites of New Orleans.

In her youth her family would spend the hot, muggy summers of St. Louis in the cool foothills of Denver as many such wealthy families did.

As the story went, when Jimmy's mother and father met, she was a beautiful outgoing woman. She had long black hair, creamy skin, and deep brown eyes. It was love match at first sight.

Jimmy knew this because his father bragged about her looks and pedigree to excess. He told anyone who would listen he'd secured the finest belle to be found from Louisiana by way of Missouri.

What she was doing with his father, Jimmy never knew or cared to understand. Maybe it was true love, or maybe it was blackmail. Either way, without her participation, Jimmy would not be here, so he thanked her for that.

Love and passion, however, was not the binding that held James Sr. and Marybeth together. What actually did cement their relationship was anyone's guess.

Jimmy wondered sometimes why no other relatives visited or when they did, why they did not stay very long. To his memory, only once or twice had he met either his mother or father's other family members. There were no more relatives besides the four of them in this strange family makeup.

From the time he was old enough to understand their roles, Jimmy's father had told his he would make sure Jimmy was educated in business and politics.

Jimmy's mother was to see to their daughter, Teresa, being properly educated in the ways of society. His father had definite plans for them both.

Teresa was prim, proper, and quite beautiful with the grace of a model. Jimmy likewise was a handsome young man, but although he had a runner's build, he was never into sports.

Jim had a scientific mind and studied those disciplines, to his father's dismay. The senior Mattock needed a son who was firmly grounded in the current political scene, not a nerd who only wanted to experiment with chemicals in the basement.

Where Jim had perfect coco-dusted skin and dark wavy hair like their father, his sister had the pale complexion of her mother with long, lustrous, black hair and hazel eyes inherited from some long-dead ancestor.

It was uncanny how Jimmy's mannerisms were just like his father's and how he shared the same temperament and condescending ways. While his sister inherited her mother's beauty and soft demeanor.

James Jr. and Teresa were not close as children, and that relationship did not blossom further as they became adults. For years he'd maintained contact with her, just in case, since he did not communicate with his father at all, but that was the extent of their connection.

Every now and then, a peculiar guilt would pass through his mind about his mother's welfare, but it was quickly erased by his own lack of attention.

Jimmy had no fond childhood memories of little league or summer camp or just growing up with his family. He didn't even have memories of Christmas toys or Thanksgiving dinners.

Jimmy couldn't recall ever playing with his sister on the lawn of the family estate. No picnics, no visits to Grandma's house, no anything that normal families, black or white, took for granted.

In fact, Jimmy found it very difficult to remember much that made him happy as a child. His only escape was into math, science, and an occasional biographical account of some scientist who lived long ago.

The Mattock's formed a timid bond that developed from living together in the same household, but they were simply acquaintances. Not even sibling rivalry disturbed their peace. It was never an issue. There was no love to compete for.

Before Jimmy knew it, Teresa was bundled off to a girl's boarding school in Boston. She only came home on holidays, which his parents never observed.

Jimmy, on the other hand, was trained by his father in all the ways of the business and political world. James Sr. expected Jimmy to go to Harvard, and that was that. He was willing to entertain Jimmy's little hobbies only to a certain point.

Jimmy, according to his father, was to be the next great senator from Colorado and eventually governor. There was no limit to how far he could go. His father was going to make sure of this.

To his father's dismay, however, Jimmy accepted the scholarship to Morehouse college, in Atlanta. Despite his father's threats and demands, Jimmy did amazingly well there.

But the Mattock legacy rested heavily upon Jimmy's back. If he wasn't doing what he was destined to—and by that, his father meant what he told Jimmy to do—by twenty-one, then all financial support would disappear. He made sure Jimmy understood this.

The elder Mattock was a self-made man. Everyone knew this because his father told his own story, over and over again, to anyone who would listen and even to those who didn't. Although from the way they lived, one would think he was from very old money.

He loved to entertain the local businesspeople and their spouses. Most of the time only white people filled the living room, but on occasion a Black family or two would be singled out and honored.

The senior Mattock always waited until everyone had eaten his prime rib and drunk his expensive wines before he launched into his tale.

It was as if he had paid someone to ask him about his childhood, no matter the audience, someone always brought it up. This was the price one paid to be on the Mattock's guest list.

Jimmy's mother and sister were forced to sit prettily and smile during these get-togethers. Jimmy was made to be his father's shadow. He was kept close at hand as a dutiful son should be. But once his father started his tales, all eyes were turned his way.

"I grew up in a tiny town about fifty miles north of Denver. I could tell you the name of the place, but it wouldn't matter. That's how pitiful it was. We lived in a rundown shack with no running water. All nine of us stayed in four rooms and not one of them was a bathroom."

"My father was a no-good bastard who beat me and my six siblings daily. Nothing we did was ever good enough. He cussed and drank cheap whiskey every chance he could get. He knew every whore in town and paraded them in front of our mother."

James Sr. would clear his throat at this point and glance around the room, making sure he held everyone's attention.

"We never knew any other family, and I guess none were ever welcomed in our home. I could only assume he got the same treatment from his father. We didn't know how he was raised, but we children all hated him and wished he would just disappear."

"Our mother, Sara, was a scared mousey little thing, who never stood up to him. She was as silent as a ghost. She rarely spoke, and when she did it was only to say, 'yes, sir' and 'no, sir.'"

His father would then take a deep drink of his expensive scotch and wait for his audience to lean forward in anticipation of his next words.

Jimmy had heard this story so many times he could recite it verbatim. The story was brought out and repeated anytime his father got on his high horse, which unfortunately was far too often. Jimmy didn't know if the story was true or not—not that it mattered anymore. It had become real to his father.

His father would continue with his prepared speech in a halting voice, as if it hurt him to remember.

"Sir, that's what we were told to call him, was a coalman on the D&L line. He always felt his color held him back. He desperately wanted to be a porter, but he knew only the high yellow, even-tempered Negroes climbed to those ranks. He certainly was not one of those in looks or temperament. He would never have done well in that position."

"Sir was midnight black with the nappiest hair this side of St. Louis. He had the rough appearance and lack of education of the lowest class of working man. The soot from the train's coal burning engine clung to his dingy clothes no matter how our mother tried to wash it out. I often felt it had penetrated deep into his very soul. You could look into his eyes and see the demons he tried so hard to conceal."

At this point in the story, the senior Mattock would walk around with his drink in his hand. He'd often would strike a pose at the fireplace with one foot on the poker stand.

He had a gold watch on a chain and would take it out to note the time. Everything about him was practiced and perfected to be as natural and nonchalant as he could make it. Most people were very impressed.

While Jimmy's mother was present, she would look on in silence with only a smile here or there to show that she was still breathing. Most of the time, she sat quietly in a corner with a glass of sweet sherry in one hand and the other hand braced on her chair as if she was ready to flee at a moment's notice.

Jimmy's father would continue with his story. "Our mother was not only silent as a ghost, but she was rarely there in mind or body. I don't know the particulars of why they were together, and I never saw what she saw in him. Maybe she was forced to be with him."

He would tell this story without an ounce of compassion in his voice, showing no love towards the woman who bore him and his siblings. One would think he was telling someone else's story instead of his own.

"Fortunately for us children, she was a buffer between us and him, the only defense we had against him. For that, I have to thank her. Anyway, I don't know why she stayed so long. He eventually beat her to death. Of course, he said she fell off the back porch and broke her neck, but the back porch was only about half a foot off the ground."

Another intentional pause was inserted here, and then, he would continue as if the weight of the world had settled around his shoulders.

"And to the rest of us, he gave little except his fists and lasting memories full of hatred. Eventually, he wandered off in one of his drunken fits and landed on the train tracks directly in front of an oncoming D&L train. We did not miss him in the least. I often thought it was a fitting end and one he certainly deserved."

By this time, his audience would shake their heads in sympathy and some naïve ladies even looked at him in a new light.

MaryBeth would sit up a little straighter because she knew James Sr. had finally reached the conclusion of his story and, in less than an hour she could go to her room. She had done her wifely duties for another night.

After everyone at the dinner party had commiserated with him on his tragic childhood and he'd puffed out his chest even more, he would continue with his tale.

James Sr. would go on to say how, with no college education and very little help, he had gone into business with just his know-how and little else.

He'd opened a store that catered to the tourist who came to ski the slopes. He carried every type of ski and camping equipment known to man.

It was rare for a Black man in the late sixties to be the owner of that type of business, but he put every penny that his creole wife's father would give him into the store.

There should have been no way it could succeed, but to the astonishment of everyone, it thrived. It went beyond even James Sr.'s wildest dreams.

By the time James Mattock Sr. unofficially retired, he had six stores spread around Colorado and interest from a national chain. He made more money in a day, so he said, than his father had made in a lifetime. But the one thing he could never attain was the respect of the white business world.

His white counterparts held seats on the local boards and were elected mayors, state representatives, and senators. That's where the big money-making decisions were made.

Try as he might, he could never reach those heights. But his son could, and James Mattock Sr. would make damn sure he did, whether he wanted it or not.

Jimmy nurtured very little love towards his family. He tolerated his abused mother and sister, realizing it was not their fault they had been born female.

But it was his father who he despised most of all. The man was a tyrant and a bully. He forced his wants and desires onto a family he held at arm's length, demanding they do as he said or else.

The senior Mattock was a man who considered himself justified in doing anything within his power to make his son succeed as he directed.

He believed wholeheartedly that the end justified his means. No matter who was hurt in the process, the senior Mattock's will was done.

All these troubling memories were polluting Jimmy's mind to the point where he gave up trying to sleep. So much had happened in the last few weeks that even he was unprepared for the majority of it, even though he had instigated most of the damaging situations.

Jimmy thought of his paternal grandfather, whom he had never met. But the way his father spoke of him was exactly how Jimmy thought of his father. The hate was a real thing passed along from generation to generation.

Although Jimmy didn't think he was anything like his father or grandfather, there did seem to be a family curse, which before this moment, he would never have believed.

The actions of Chrystal, Bryan and the rest of his family attested to the fact that much was going on that was out of his control. It was as if an evil voodoo priestess had personally visited him and his family and cursed them all with eternal damnation on earth.

His last thoughts before sleep finally claimed him were of destroying the curse and regaining control by destroying the man who started it. He would get rid of his father, James Mattock Sr., if it was the last thing he ever did. In fact, he had an idea forming in his brain as blessed sleep brought a smile to his face.

THE WAITING ROOM

Back in the hospital's waiting room Jimmy's family gathered. Bryan tried to lead them as far away as possible from the other occupants in the room. He knew from experience that the conversation they were getting ready to have would be something unfit for stranger's ears.

With a shaky hand, Mrs. Mattock wiped a handkerchief across her ashen face. She stood in the shadow of her husband as Royce steered Jessica to a chair to sit.

James Sr. captured his wife around her waist and sat her next to the wall. Mrs. Mattock wrung her slim hands as she asked Bryan a question.

"Why is James so hostile? I mean, he was so much better the other night before we left. I finally thought we were making progress. What happened to make him this way--so, so angry?"

Bryan shook with agitation and dropped in a chair across from her.

"He's . . . well, he's just being himself, his usual. hard headed, stubborn self. We did have a bit of shocking news after you two left, and things kind of got out of control with his temper."

"I told you Becky, that something like this was going on." The senior Mattock huffed as if he had run an ill-timed marathon, and he pronounced the nickname he had for his wife, Becky, with disdain.

"James Jr. does not want to act in a humane and decent way. Like a mature upstanding man would. He's hard headed and selfish."

The other occupants of the waiting room looked up from their conversations as James Sr.'s voice grew louder. A couple stood and headed for the door to escape the crazed scene unfolding in front of them.

James Sr. noticed the people leaving and smirked as he continued speaking in a rough voice. "I think the fool probably did this on purpose, trying to garner sympathy from you and everyone else."

With those words, James Sr. sat down in one of the uncomfortable waiting room chairs beside his wife and crossed his legs. He looked around at Bryan, Royce and Jessica and shook his head in triumph as if to say, *I told you he was a monster and now you have to see it too.*

No one rose to his bait, and the elder Mattock looked around in confusion. With most of his audience gone or failing to react, he stood up again and proclaimed loudly to his unfortunate family.

"He's always been this way. Even as a boy, he played games with your affection. I told you Becky, not to put too much hope into his words. It's always been and always will be that a man's actions show you what he's made of."

James Sr. harrumphed and crossed his arms across his chest as if the conversation was closed.

"I don't care what you say James. He's my son, and I will not give up on him. Whatever is going on to make him act like this can be fixed. I know it can."

"Becky, you will never learn. Some men can't be helped. You have to want to change. All your wanting for them won't change a damn thing."

"I didn't give up on you. If you can change, have the 'want to,' then my son can too. There's no one more stubborn than you, James."

Jessica turned to Royce with a sad smile on her face. Royce gave her the same answering smile as he stood and patted his grandmother's shoulder. He was about to say something when his grandmother spoke up again.

MaryBeth turned her attention from her husband to Bryan. "Bryan I need your help. We are going to save my son, and I will not give up. No one, James, can make me turn my back on my only son."

Bryan gasped at her words. He looked from Royce to Jessica and back again to MaryBeth. Finally, he answered her with wet eyes and a choked voice.

"Mrs. Mattock, I want nothing more than to fix Jim, as you say. But I have tried everything I know to get him to change this disastrous path he's on." Bryan hesitated, dropped his head, shuddering all over.

"See, my dear, I told you so. Even the man, um, he's supposed to be involved with doesn't see a way to deal with his crazy antics."

James Sr. tried to catch his wife's hand, but MaryBeth pulled away from him. He continued on as if his wife had done no such thing.

"Your son is finally getting what he deserves. I have used up the last of my good will towards him, and if you know what's good for you all, you all will give up on him also. Good riddance to him."

MaryBeth turned her back to her husband and gazed at the wall as if she was in a trance.

James Sr. paid no attention to his wife's reaction. "I can only imagine what Bryan has been through with your son. Like I said, a man's actions speak for him. James Jr. is playing a dangerous game, and I will not allow him to continue to hurt you Becky. I don't know about the rest of you, but I'm finished with this nonsense. In fact it's time to return to our hotel room. He made it clear we were—what was that word? Oh yes, he said we were *dismissed*."

James Sr. stood, knocking over his chair and eliciting gasps from Jessica and MaryBeth. Bryan looked to Royce, pleading with his eyes for Royce to say something to diffuse this volatile situation. But not even Royce, the peacemaker, could come up with anything to clear the anger and disappointment from the room.

"Come on Becky. Let me help you up." James Sr. reached for her hand, but she swatted it away.

"Don't you dare touch me. I can't believe the things you just said. I will never give up on him, and if you don't want to help me, I'll just help him myself. I'll get the help I need even if I have to go through you, James, to reach my son, the son you have obviously disowned."

"Becky, stop this nonsense. I'm leaving and you're coming with me."

"No, James, I am not. And stop calling me Becky. I hate that stupid nickname. Bryan, let's go. I've had enough of the foul air in here."

Bryan helped a hostile looking MaryBeth from her seat. As he stepped around Mr. Mattock Bryan turned to Royce and said, "I guess I'll see you later. Mrs. Mattock is ready to go."

Mr. James Mattock Sr. smirked at his wife as she exited with Bryan. "This isn't over. It's not over until I say so and, I. Haven't. Said. So. Yet."

CHAPTER 9

Royce ushered Jessica into their small condominium, where he closed and locked the door for the night. He looked back at his wife, who had flopped down on the sofa in defeat.

The drive home from the hospital had been shrouded in a gloomy malaise. Neither Royce nor Jessica brought up the subject that dominated both their minds.

Finally, as if an unspoken agreement had sealed their lips until now, they both spoke their thoughts out loud.

"What in the nine levels of hell was that all about?" Royce asked.

"You don't even have to say it. Your dad is such a piece of work. I underestimated the level of crazy that had taken over his mind." Jessica shook her head as she leaned back into the sofa.

"It seems everybody, and I mean everybody, has lost their ever-loving minds. I mean Dad is so—I don't even know . . ."

Royce dropped heavily onto the sofa beside Jessica and pulled her close. "I feel like so much of this is my fault. If I hadn't invited Eric to the wedding in the first place, then Mom wouldn't have fainted and been embarrassed by Eric showing up. Then they wouldn't have had the showdown. And then the awful way the truth came out."

"Stop it. You can go on and on about the 'Ifs' and 'thens' and still not cover it all. Look. Your parents are adults, and they made the decisions to do what they did. Be thankful because if they hadn't, you and I would not be sitting here right now."

Royce ran his hand over his hair and exhaled loudly. "Yeah, you're right, and I know they are ultimately responsible for their actions. It's just Dad is so far gone with the crazy stuff he's been doing. It makes me sick to think about what Chrystal told us."

"I know, right? To think he wanted to hurt your mom and Eric so badly that he tried to get thugs to do his nasty business. Eric being your biological father still doesn't excuse your dad's actions."

"I just knew something crazy was going to happen, but never in my wildest dreams did I think this kind of bullshit was going to hit the fan." Royce dropped his head to the back of the sofa and stilled.

"No matter what your mom did or didn't do, her actions do not warrant this type of retaliation. I know it's hard to hold on to any positive feelings towards him, but that doesn't mean you've stopped caring about him. Right? Right?"

"I don't know what I think anymore. It's crazy, just so bizarre. I can't put into words just how I feel about him. He wasn't around much after their divorce, and frankly, he wasn't that much of a hands-on dad before that. But I respected him because he was my mother's husband, my father, not because he showed me much love. It was all I knew to do."

"Oh, Royce. I know it was difficult growing up in that family, but you had your grandparents, Chrystal, and your Mom. Like you told me, you even remember Eric coming around. Their love had to cover you, or you wouldn't be the man you are today."

"Well, I guess so. But you can't reason with Dad now if you ever could. But now, the way he talks and acts towards us all scares me."

"But he did come around when you all were younger. You said he reached out to you and Chrystal after Jewell was born. It sounds like he maybe wanted to be in you guys' lives. Right?"

Jessica looked deeply into Royce's eyes as she tried to gauge his reactions to her words.

"You know, it always seemed like an act he was putting on. It never felt genuine. When he sent a car for us to come over, it was like he was interrogating us, not just spending time with his kids. You know, pumping us for info about Mom. It was hush-hush too. He made it plain we were not to tell Mom. I still feel guilty about those years. "

"I guess I always thought you didn't talk about your dad much because there wasn't much to tell. Now I see there was too much stuff going on. It's like one of those crazy reality shows. I feel like I'll hear the "dun dun da dun" music any moment," especially when we were in the waiting room with your grandparents and Bryan, the air was thick with pain."

Royce reached for Jessica's hand and brought it to his lips for a small kiss.

"Yeah I know. Grandfather is so hostile towards Dad. Likewise, there's no love lost from Dad's side either. I wonder what it must have felt like growing up in his family. We never had much to do with them. I only remember them coming to town maybe twice."

Jessica laid her hand on Royce's leg and squeezed gently. He looked at her with love in his eyes.

"But your grandmother is so sweet. I wanted to cheer her on when she stood up to your grandfather. She was not kidding about her son. And then when she told him to stop calling her that stupid nickname Becky, I wanted to laugh out loud. She is one feisty little lady."

"And that's strange too. Because this trip is the first time I've ever heard more than a few words from her. The other day when she stood up to grandfather about Bryan and Dad being in love, was super stellar. I love her a lot more for finally speaking up. I guess she's tired of the stress these Mattock men has caused her too."

Jessica laughed at Royce's comment. "That's a good thing. As I said before and will say again before all this is through, you Mattock's are some tough people to get along with. But I love you, so I'll let you slide."

I'm going to call Mom and Chrystal and let them know what happened at the hospital."

Royce left the sofa and moved into the small kitchen. "I'm going to get a soda to wet my throat. Want anything?"

Jessica came into the kitchen and leaned on the counter. "Naw, I'm good. I want to hear what you're going to tell your family, so I'm sticking close to you to support you."

"Thank you baby, for, well, everything. You didn't have to come to the hospital and all, but I'm glad you did."

"Now, you know it's only been a couple of weeks of married life, so it's too soon to step away from you. You don't know how to act married yet." Jessica laughed as she swatted Royce on the butt.

Royce grabbed her around the waist and kissed her hard. "You right about that. And you know another thing."

"Probably so, because I'm gifted that way, knowing everything about you," Jessica smiled.

"Okay then. I love you, Mrs. Jessica Mattock, and you can't do a thing about it."

"I love you too, Mr. Royce Mattock, and I wouldn't have it any other way."

They hugged each other in a tight hold. Jessica pulled back first and spoke.

"And to tell you the truth, I don't blame Chrystal for not coming to see your father. After the way she and Bryan said he acted towards her and Tyler, well just let me say, I don't think I'd be coming around either to see his ass."

Royce laughed at Jessica's words. "Okay then, let's get this call over with so we can go to bed. All I want to do is hold you all night long, loving you and forgetting about the mess my parents have made with their lives. What they've done is over and done with. We'll push on and have love in our lives regardless of the mistakes of the past. Are you with me, bae?"

"I'll always be with you. No matter what comes from any direction. I got you, just like I know you got me. Come on, let's get this call done and get on to that good loving part."

CHAPTER 10

It was past ten o'clock before Chrystal finished putting all three children down for the night. She and Tyler worked efficiently together, bathing and settling them down for a good night's sleep.

The children's room contained two toddler beds for Jewell and Oro and a crib for Jade. The arrangement worked very well for them all. No child wanted to sleep alone, so they all occupied the same room to be close to one another if they woke up.

Tyler, bless his heart, read them a story from Jewell's favorite book, *Leighanne and Her Magical Growing Shoes.* Jade, being so young, didn't pay much attention to the words of the story. She was happy just to be near her papa and her brother and sister, looking at the pictures.

Tyler was turning out to be such a wonderful dad. Chrystal didn't know what she would do if Tyler left her and tried to take Jade with him. He would be justified if he ever found out she had sexual relations with that piece of shit Smoke.

She just hoped and prayed that part of her life never came to full light. If Tyler left her now, she didn't think she would be strong enough to take it.

Thinking about the mistakes she made while she was living that messy lifestyle made her shudder. What a fool she had been, trusting her cousin Nikki. Carrying dope around and dealing with Duck, the biggest trap king and pimp around-- made her heart ache at her own stupidity.

Chrystal's mind returned to the encounter she'd endured just a few short days ago. She replayed the crazy conversation she had with Nikki in the small bathroom at her rental.

"Nik, what's going on?" Chrystal had asked. "Why'd you take the money from the package you gave me to give to Duck them? You must've known Smoke was going to blame me."

Nikki had slowly looked up at Chrystal. "Yeah, that's why I did it. You got everything. You're smart and got a slamming body. You got a great family, you're beautiful, and everybody want you, including Smoke. I ain't got nothing worth nothing. All Smoke did was talk about you day and night. I wanted to make you look bad. I wanted Smoke to be mad at you. I wanted to be the one he turned to."

Shock and disbelief has washed over Chrystal. "What?! Girl, please. You know how messed up my life has been. I got three babies by three different guys and not one of them in sight. How the hell do you think I got it going on? You're a lot better off than me. You only have yourself to worry about. I got me and three kids."

Nikki, who always made jokes and wisecracks, was at the lowest point in her life. She didn't want to, but Chrystal felt sorry for her cousin even though Nikki had brought all this mess down onto her own head.

"Look, I'm trying to understand. We've been girls for a long time, but I'm not taking the blame for this. What did you do with the money?"

"I still got the money. I ain't that stupid, but if Smoke find out I took it, he'll beat me to death."

Nikki said as she rocked back and forth on the toilet.

"I'm sorry, okay? I didn't think it would end up like this. I just wanted to shine like you, for once. All I did was end up being used and left at the curb like week-old garbage. I know you won't believe it, but I love you. You my girl. You all I got." Nikki shuddered as big liquid drops of misery fell from her eyes.

It just proved blood was not thicker than water and now that water ran as cold as ice through Chrystal's veins. Deep in the bosom of family was not the blessed haven everyone made it out to be. Betrayal was a mother to get over.

There was no reason to borrow trouble, as her grandmother always said, but she couldn't help it. When she tried to take control of her own life, everything collapsed around her. And when she let others guide her, the results were worse than if she had followed her own heart. What the hell was she to do?

Chrystal slowly turned off the overhead light, leaving a nightlight on in the corner. She looked back one last time at all three children and hugged her arms around herself. She was still troubled and knew more trouble was coming soon.

Her mother's boyfriend and Royce's father Eric, had arrived that afternoon. Her mother had whisked Chrystal and Eric to the clinic to get a DNA test. The results would be ready tomorrow.

Chrystal had to agree with her mother that Jimmy was probably lying about only Royce being Eric's child. It just didn't seem right otherwise.

As for Eric, to say he was pissed was an understatement. Eric was ready to commit murder.

Jackie had filled him in on all the craziness that Jimmy had done to everyone in the last few days. The story started with Jimmy's ridiculous, sadistic behavior on Friday night and ended with his absurd hospital stay from drinking too much whiskey. Her father was a piece of work to the nth degree.

Chrystal could hear them all the way down the hall from the family room. Her mother was praying the DNA test would be the final nail in Jimmy's coffin. She'd told Eric, her mother, and sister that she knew he was a liar, and therefore, Jimmy had to be lying about Chrystal's paternity.

Eric was loud and extremely angry. He told Jackie if Jimmy were here right now, he would finally strangle all the shit out of him.

Chrystal would never have believed she would say this, but she hoped her mother was right and Jimmy was not her biological father. Right that moment, she felt anyone would be better than James "Jimmy" Mattock Jr.

It would be payback if Eric would go ahead and whip his butt for all the lies, manipulation, and dangerous situations he placed them all in. That would give him something to take back to his house so he would remember for the last time not to mess over them.

And to top off a really shitty day, Royce and Jessica had called to fill them in on the mess that happened at the hospital. Now that was the craziest stuff Chrystal had ever heard.

To think that her grandparents had come to the hospital and her grandfather had gotten into a fight with Jimmy was almost too funny. Then, Royce said, they had another tell-all in the waiting room after the doctor told them to leave Jimmy's room.

And if that wasn't enough, Grandmother told Grandfather off and told him not to call her that ugly nickname, Becky. For her to leave with Bryan must have been the icing on the cake.

She had to give it to her grandmother; she was one spicy old lady. Chrystal laughed to herself just thinking about the look that must have been on grandfather's face.

Now she needed to get herself together and woman up. Wasting time in the kids' room didn't help anything. For once in her life, she had to own up to her own bullshit. *Okay, I guess it's time to face the music before Tyler comes back looking for me,* she thought.

She and Tyler were going back to her rental to spend the night. It didn't feel right for them to bed down together in her grandmother's house. Some things, she believed, should be kept out of her grandmother's home.

Besides, they had never gotten the chance to celebrate their engagement the proper way. She prayed for a good rest of her Saturday night, even though she didn't feel much like celebrating. What she really needed was a good cuddling and plenty of relaxing sleep.

Chrystal slowly closed the door to the children's room and leaned on the hallway wall. To say she was exhausted was an understatement. She had never felt so small and helpless as she did when talking to her father late last night.

"God help me," she mumbled quietly, "but I hate him so much. I wish he had never come back into my life."

All the things he had done and the ways he manipulated her made her stomach ache. She had been so foolish, thinking he had her best interest at heart, thinking he actually loved her. He'd essentially turned her against her own mother.

And to think he and her cousin Nikki were working behind the scenes to derail her life every chance they got. To top it all off, there was the sordid relationship between Jimmy, Nikki, Smoke and Duck. Still letting her mind linger on the last conversation with Nikki and Smoke made her want to vomit.

Chrystal had shaken her head at Smoke and pulled the package of money out of her big bag.

"I want you to acknowledge that I gave you the ten thousand dollars you said you lost from your dealings with Duck. I want you to write paid in full across the bottom and sign your government name, Calvin Dotson. Is that clear enough for you?"

Nikki had stared at Smoke for a long moment. "Come on Smoke. Me and Chrystal got things to do. Let's do this so we can go."

Smoke stared right back as if he couldn't believe Nikki was standing up to him. "You must have smoked too many rocks, Nik. Who you think you talking to?"

Smoke looked from Nikki to Chrystal. "I swear, I ain't never gonna mess with you two crazy-ass bitches again."

Chrystal had looked at Smoke, wondering how she ever let Nikki talk her into a disgusting, foul relationship with him.

"Give me that damn piece of paper so I can write your shit-ass note. You just as crazy as yo old man. Always wanting us to beat up anybody who look at you twice. It's a good thing me and Duck ain't got time to hit your mama and her boyfriend. I'm tired of all that bullshit."

Chrystal was handing Smoke the paper and pen from her bag when his last comments stopped her short. "What the hell you talking about? Who did you beat up, and what about my mama?"

Nikki nervously edged towards the front door. "Come on, Chrystal. Let's go. He just talking trash."

"Wait a minute, Nikki. I want to hear this trash he got to say." Chrystal watched Smoke as he took the paper and pen and wrote something.

"What do somebody like you, know about my family?"

Smoke had a smug look on his face as he gave Chrystal back the paper and answered her.

"I know a lot mo' than you bitch. Yo crazy-ass daddy wanted that foreign guy that knocked you up to disappear out of his precious baby's life. Remember about four years ago? We made it happen. So now he pissed at yo mama, so he wanted her and her new boyfriend to have a little accident. But we ain't got time for shit like that no more."

"You lying! My daddy would never do that. He would never hire you and Duck to hurt my mother."

Chrystal didn't want to believe what Smoke was telling her. But she had gone to her father about Omar, and right after that, Omar disappeared. She was so distraught at the time, and afterwards with Oro's birth, she never bothered to ask her father what happened to Omar.

But to hurt her mother and Eric, that was just too damn much.

"Come on, Chrystal. Let's go. We did what we came to do. Let's go."

Nikki pulled on Chrystal's arm while Smoke looked at them both and laughed like a crazy man.

Chrystal had sat quietly on the train ride home. Nikki kept apologizing as she tried to get Chrystal's attention.

"I'm so sorry," Nikki said. "What do I have to do to make this up to you? I swear I never meant to hurt you. Your daddy said it was to protect you, and I wanted to help. You my bestie. You all I got."

Nikki wiped her eyes. She told Chrystal how Jimmy come to her, asking about sketchy people who would do shady shit. She'd turned him on to Smoke and Duck and left the details to them to work out.

"I swear I didn't know what he had planned for Omar. But I knew you were scared and unhappy. I just wanted to help. And that stuff with your mama them, that's just foul. I would never-- "

"Shut up, Nikki. I don't want to hear anything else from you. I'm so mad right now that I want to whip your stupid ass."

Chrystal came back to the present in her thoughts. Tears gathered in her eyes, scarlet tears of frustration and disappointment. She'd always thought her father had her back. But this was too much. This was the ultimate betrayal.

Why did he want to hurt her mother so badly? All these years, Chrystal had blamed her mother for her sorry life, thinking her father was the one who was misunderstood and ill used by her mother.

And to think she had lain down with that piece of filth, Smoke, over and over. Doing whatever he told her to do to make a couple of dollars. A bitter taste rose in her throat. How could she have been so blind, so naïve, as to trust her father and Nikki?

It's way past time for me to get myself together. I'm the only one who can control my life, and damn if

THE DARKEST GREY

I'm going to let Daddy or anybody else control me anymore.

Okay, this is the last time
The last time I try to clear the air
The last time I try to understand
Okay, the last time I say this

My heart breaks that you don't want to talk
You tell me that I'm making too much of this
You tell me to let it go and move on
Okay, I won't speak it aloud any more

But . . . just because I won't speak on it
Just because the words don't leave my mouth
Just because it hurts you too much
Okay, I'll hold it all inside my head

I burst with the unspoken mess inside me
I choke on the words held behind my teeth
I feel like my trust is totally broken
Okay, this is the last time I cry because of you

The only answer to everyone's number-one problem is to remove him from our lives. If he wasn't here then, he couldn't tell me what to do anymore. The problem now is how to get rid of him for the last time. As he always said, the end always justifies the means.

CHAPTER 11

Bryan Denveue was saying goodnight to his distraught houseguest. They'd stopped at the mall on the way home to pick up some necessities for her.

They'd chatted nervously about inconsequential things on the drive home. It wasn't an uneasy ride, just two people lost in their own thoughts. Now that they were home, maybe things would be more settled.

"Mrs. Mattock I hope you'll be comfortable here. I always imagined this suite for our special guests, but Jim and I hardly ever have guests stay."

Mrs. Mattock carelessly threw her Louboutin purse on a side chair, and dropped the bag of necessities on the bed. "Don't worry, Bryan. And please call me MaryBeth. This is a beautiful room, and I can feel the love you've put into decorating it. It's full of your bright happy attitude."

Bryan looked around the room. Mrs. Mattock or MaryBeth, as she wanted to be called, was standing in as she complimented him so enthusiastically. He also remembered how Jim begrudgingly, helped him pick through the samples for bedding, curtains, towels, and carpeting.

Bryan had visited showrooms, dragging a fussing Jim with him, to find the perfect furnishings and choose a complementary wall color. Now, it was all for what?

The thought of Jim's behavior towards him and his family made Bryan physically ill. The disrespect he showed to his own mother was unforgivable.

However, Jim's reaction to his father was understandable. He understood all too well the cold-hearted hatred Jim had for Mr. Mattock and vice versa. In fact, Bryan felt the same as Jim did about Mr. Mattock, but Jim's mother was a different issue altogether.

In many ways, MaryBeth was like Bryan's own mother. Loving sweetness and kindness came naturally to both women. No matter what Bryan had done or how misguided he had been, his mother always had his back.

Sadly, he realized he hadn't talked to his mom in two weeks, in fact since the wedding. It made him a little ashamed to realize this, and as soon as he was finished with MaryBeth, he would give his mom a call. He understood a mother's love for her child was eternal.

"Bryan, this is so nice and comfortable, but you don't have to continue to oversee me. I'm all right now that I've seen and heard James Jr. for myself. You've been such a wonderful man and I have nothing but love for you. But there is one thing I would like for you to answer me truthfully."

Bryan cringed. He thought he knew what Mrs. Mattock was going to ask him, and he didn't know if he could answer her truthfully.

"Exactly what is the relationship between James and his ex-wife Jackie? He said she was fine but out of his life, but there seems to be something going on between you all. Almost as if he's hiding something."

Bryan was taken aback. That wasn't what he imagined her asking. He'd thought she wanted to know if he still loved Jim after all this messy situation her son had gotten them into.

"I-I don't know what you mean. What are you asking me?" Bryan rubbed his hand over his rapidly thinning hair. His mind ran in loops as he sought an answer to a question he didn't want to answer. He snatched a pillow from the bed and hugged it to his chest.

"Well, every time James or I mention Jackie's name, it's as if everyone is holding their collective breath. What's really going on? What's the secret you all are trying to not let out the bag? What are you not telling me? And where's Chrystal? I don't understand why she didn't come to see her father."

MaryBeth's eyes sparkled with unshed tears as she looked sincerely into Bryan's eyes.

"MaryBeth, I don't know what to say. There's been a lot of tension since Royce and Jessica's wedding. You know how families can be, especially since Jim and Jackie are divorced. It may not have been the most congenial reunion between the two, but there's not much to tell."

Bryan held his breath, hoping the lie he was telling wouldn't come back to haunt him. But mostly he prayed his answer was good enough to settle her mind about Jim and Jackie.

"That answers some of my questions but, why hasn't Chrystal shown up? Come to think of it, Bryan, she seemed to be openly hostile towards James when we were here the other day."

"Nothing's going on. It's just like I said. Some family issues that just became known, and Jim wasn't that happy about it."

Bryan wrung his hands, then hugged the pillow and hung his head. He felt horrible about the run around he was giving Jim's mother. But there was no way he could tell her the truth.

"Were you the cause of their breakup? Or did James do something else horrible to Jackie? He's much too much like his father. A father who is mean, manipulative, and obsessive about what one can do or not." MaryBeth looked to be in another world as she continued slowly.

"He is a man; I have known my entire adult life and still don't understand if he is even capable of love for anyone other than himself. I wish I had stood up to James's father. I wish I'd had enough strength to--"

Bryan looked wide eyed at MaryBeth. *What's with all the disclosures about Jim's father?* He wondered where this was leading and why. Was her life just as miserable as his had become? These Mattock men were impossible to keep on loving.

"Look, you don't have to confide in me about your husband. I understand that yes, he and Jim are very much alike, but I—"

"Please listen to me. I imagine this rambling conversation I'm dumping on you is a lot, but let me finish. I am not that gullible or delicate as my husband tries to make you believe. James and his sister, Teresa, talk now and then. She was the one who told us about Royce and Jessica's wedding, as you know. She also told me James had been unhappy with his and Jackie's marriage for years. For you, his frat brother, to suddenly turn into his love interest could not have just happened overnight."

"Mrs. Mattock, I don't want to discuss what Jim and Jackie's marriage problems have been. I don't believe it's my place to do so."

"You're wrong, Bryan and I told you to call me MaryBeth."

"MaryBeth, I don't feel comfortable talking about Jim's feelings for Jackie. And I couldn't possibly tell you about the rest."

"It's very much your place to help me understand what's wrong with James. Whether or not you feel comfortable with this situation you find yourself in, it's just part of loving one of these Mattock men. So I can tell James is suffering and so are you."

"But what you don't understand." Bryan stuttered to a halt as MaryBeth waved her hand sharply to stop his words.

"That's what I'm asking you to do now, to try to understand. I want to know what has happened to turn my son into this selfish, tortured man. I know you love him. I see it in your eyes. I hear it in your voice. I know how it is to love someone like him."

Bryan took MaryBeth's cold hands in his, but he looked down at his feet.

"Mrs., uh, MaryBeth, I understand your feelings, but again, I don't have answers to your questions. I certainly don't have answers that will make it better for you to understand what is going on here. I feel like anything I say will only make things much worse."

"Bryan, please. I'm begging you to help me. There's nothing you could say that will turn me away from my son and the people he loves. Please help me to help you all. I have been too silent in the past, and look where that has gotten us. I feel if I had said something, done something, James wouldn't have suffered so."

"All right," Bryan said reluctantly. "You want an answer that will make everything clearer, but there is no one answer. This thing, this tragedy we find ourselves in, is so multi-layered. There are many, many—"

"Just spit it out!. As I said, I'm not so delicate or fragile that the truth will stop my heart. I have seen and experienced more ugliness in my dealings with James's father than you would ever believe."

Bryan dropped his hands to his side in defeat. "Okay but remember you asked for this information."

"I understand and thank you for sharing what you know."

"Hmm, well, Jim married Jackie because your husband threatened him with disinheritance."

MaryBeth gasped and covered her mouth with her hand.

Bryan continued in a singsong rushed voice. "He only married Jackie as a ruse to appease your husband, not because he was in love with her. He and I have been together as a couple since we met in college. I think Jackie knew this and sought true love elsewhere. We have recently come to find out Royce definitely isn't Jim's biological child and Chrystal might not be."

MaryBeth sat on the end of the bed with a sigh. "All right, thank you for that information. I think I understand what you're saying. So Jim found out this information recently and wasn't happy about it. I can understand that also."

MaryBeth trembled slightly and wiped at her brow while tears silently fell from her eyes.

Bryan handed her some tissues from the box on the nightstand.

"I'm sorry to say he wasn't just unhappy. He went ballistic. He . . . The truth is he placed a hit on Jackie and her lover, who Royce had invited to his wedding without understanding the situation. Jim, I'm sorry to say, has deceived us all in so many ways, and I actually left him after we had a terrible fight. I only came back this afternoon to check on him after he drank himself into a stupor."

"No Bryan! Oh, no! You've shocked me more than I could have imagined. What in the world has been going on? Why would he do that?"

"He's become mentally unstable. He blames everything on Jackie and her lover, Eric. He blames them for things that never even happened. Chrystal found out about his despicable behavior and demanded he stop and come clean with her mother. He refused her demands, and they had a horrible fight. Chrystal's fiancé came with her to confront Jim, and Jim all but kicked him out of the house after accusing him of being a deadbeat dad."

MaryBeth tore the tissue into little pieces as she sat stoically on the bed. "I'm sorry I asked. I never thought it could get this bad. Your Jim is very much like his father. It seems history does repeat itself."

Bryan looked over her head to a scenic picture on the opposite wall, wondering what her cryptic words meant.

"You would know better than I what happened between Jim and his father growing up. Even in adulthood, Jim carried the weight of being his father's son heavily on his unsupported shoulders."

"Well, I think I have a better idea of what's going on now. You are remarkably brave to have stayed this long. It seems we also are very much alike in believing love can conquer all."

"It's been a lot of years," Bryan said, "and no, not all of them good, but Jim and I connected from the first day we met. There has many a time when I wanted to end the relationship. And being brave was not the reason why I didn't."

MaryBeth sighed. "Yes, I'm sure bravery is not the only reason. Like me, you've suffered so long you don't know any other way to live. My husband destroyed me. He took the best parts of who I was and ground me under his tyrannical heels. What little bit of myself I somehow salvaged barely maintains me."

Bryan stooped down onto the colorful rug and took MaryBeth's hands into his own.

"MaryBeth, I care for you as if you were my own mother. I hate being in this situation more than you'll ever know, but I can't keep on doing this. I can't just stand by and let Jim destroy his and everyone else's lives. I just can't."

"You're right, Bryan, and like you, I can't let James destroy the little love I have left in this world.

A ringing startled MaryBeth, but she looked at Bryan without moving.

Bryan quietly said, "I think that's your cell ringing."

"Yes, yes, I believe you're right. Let me get it."

Bryan grabbed MaryBeth's purse. "Here it is."

Hesitantly, as if she feared a poisonous snake was nestled in her bag, she pulled out the cell phone. "Hello James."

Bryan turned his back and walked to the window to give her some privacy, but he couldn't help but hear her side of the conversation.

"I'm fine and you? No I'll see you tomorrow, that is if you come to the hospital. If not, then I suppose I'll see you at home."

Bryan played with the thick wooden blinds at the window as he guessed the other side of the conversation going on behind him. *He must be trying to force her back to his side. If nothing else, tonight I've learned that MaryBeth is no pushover.*

"If that's how you feel, then so be it. I'm going to stay here until James is released from the hospital. Hmm, no. I do realize he is my son, as you say. There's never been a moment you didn't remind me of that. Feel free to do whatever you want. I don't see how this is any different from your past actions. Whatever. Goodbye."

MaryBeth clicked off her phone and slowly stood up from her seated position on the bed. She placed the phone back in her purse and robotically shuffled towards the ensuite bathroom.

Bryan turned from the window and fidgeted with his hands. "Are you all right, MaryBeth? Do you need anything else to help you rest?"

"Ha! By that, do you mean something to help me pretend that all this is just a dream, some terrible nightmare? Otherwise, no, I don't think you have what I need to keep me from wanting my husband dead."

CHAPTER 12

Jackie Mattock woke to strong arms surrounding her. The weekend had started out like a Hollywood disaster movie, but now Eric was holding her, and her heart had finally stopped racing.

She wanted to pretend it was all a dream, but as usual, life just didn't want her to have happily ever after. Except, of course, for Eric being back in her life, it stunk to high heaven.

It was still dark in her bedroom, as dawn was still a few hours away. A murky light shone through the violet curtains from the streetlights on the corner.

She had been dreaming, but the details were scattering from her mind like wind-blown leaves. All she really knew now, was the dream had been disturbing and left her feeling more uneasy as ever.

"What ya thinking?" Eric asked in a gruff voice. "And don't tell me 'nothing' because I feel how you just tensed up."

"How did you know I was awake? I could've been playing possum all along." Jackie stretched in Eric's arms and snuggled closer to his side.

"Yeah, right, I've been holding you for a while, and you were relaxed and limber. Now you're thinking too much about all this Jimmy nonsense, and your back is as stiff as granite."

Jackie struggled to see Eric in the minimal light, but she could feel the concern coming off him in waves. "Well, I can't help but worry. I want those results from the test right now. When do you think they'll come through?"

She tried to hold on to the last smidgens of sleep to pull the dream back into her mind, but it escaped again.

"Listen, my darling. First of all, it's O-dark-thirty in the morning, and those test results are probably not ready yet. And second and most importantly, I don't care what those tests say. It won't change a thing about how I see you or the kids. I love you now and before, the same way, whether or not I am Chrystal's biological dad."

"But Eric—"

"No buts. You guys are all mine, no matter what the tests say. I just want you to relax and not worry about your crazy ex. He's had too much of an influence on everyone's emotions and lives as it is. And it's not a good thing. In fact it's a very fucked-up thing."

"I know, I know. I just want things to go back to some sort of normal. This last month has aged me a good ten years. My heart races every time the phone rings or someone knocks on the door. I don't know if I should laugh or cry. It's scary, and now, after Royce told us about what happened at the hospital, it sounds like Jimmy and his damn father are out of their freaking minds."

"Yes, it certainly seems that way. But you know what's funny about all this?"

"No, I don't." Jackie scooted even closer to Eric's side so that he could hug her to his chest.

"Well it seems that Jimmy and his father are two of a kind, while his mother turns out to be a dragon."

Jackie smiled to herself and stifled a yawn. "Yeah, the thought of his mother actually telling his father off does bring a smile to my face. I never knew she had it in her. But you know you can even push an angel to do the devil's work. And since son and father are two of a kind, it's easy for them to push someone to that extreme."

"Right you are, my lovely lady. Okay, so what are we going to do later today? I don't want to just sit around waiting for those test results to pop up on the site. We need to be proactive. In fact I think we need to be ready to go to the hospital and confront your ex just as soon as possible. Hit him with the facts, hit him hard. Hit him repeatedly with the truth."

"I like that idea. Hit him while he's down, and then stomp his crazy-ass head into the ground."

Eric laughed out loud at Jackie's words. "I like your mindset. I like it a lot and I'm going to make sure I wear my steel toed boots."

He squeezed Jackie. "But first, since you woke me up with all that tension running through your body, I think I need a little something-something to help me relax and go back to sleep."

"So now you're blaming me for waking you, huh?"

"Yes, I am. So what are you going to do about it, my lovely?"

Jackie rubbed Eric's chest and whispered, "I guess I'll just have to get you in the right mood again. It seems you're insatiable."

Eric chuckled and grabbed Jackie's hand. "Yes, I am. Here, let me give you a deep-tissue massage, and then we'll see who's insatiable or not."

Jackie laughed quietly. "All right, Mr. Greedy. Get to massaging right now."

CHRYSTAL AND TYLER

Chrystal woke with a jolt, startled out of sleep by a nightmare. She sat up in bed, catching her breath as if she'd been chased over a long distance. Sweat beaded on her brow. Her heart lurched in her chest and frosty, ragged breaths issued from her mouth.

"What's the matter baby? Why are you breathing so hard?" Tyler pulled Chrystal back down to the bed.

"I don't know. I was dreaming, I think. But something terrible was chasing me. Something cold, dark, and deadly was just about to grab me."

"It's all right. I got you. I'm right here. Don't worry."

Chrystal reached out and tangled her fingers with Tyler's and sighed. "It was so real. I couldn't get away. It was like this thing was going to eat me up and spit out my bones." She shuddered hard as she lay her head on Tyler's chest.

"It's just your mind trying to come to terms with all this mess about your dad. It's no wonder you were having nightmares about him. According to what Royce told us, your dad is way out there in never-never land."

"Yeah, I guess so. But, Bae, what if something else is going on. I mean Ms. Sylvi always said that dreams were a gateway to a different reality. Ugh! I hate to think that thing that I felt is out there somewhere."

"Chrystal, stop it. You're overreacting. And it's still dark outside. It was just a dream, not an omen or something. Let's go back to sleep. It seems like we're going to have a long day ahead of us."

"I know you're right, but ..."

"Shh, just close your eyes and relax. I'm right here and I dare anything to come between us. I love you and I'm never letting you go. So hush, baby, and sleep. Let tomorrow take care of itself."

Chrystal yawned and nodded her head. "Okay, you're right. Let tomorrow take care of tomorrow."

But her mind was reeling with the what-ifs, and she knew more strangeness was out there than they could have ever imagined.

CHAPTER 13

Jimmy Mattock came drowsily awake to a strong sensation of wrongness. He kept his eyes closed as he assessed his situation. The air he breathed in and out of his lungs felt much too cold and foreboding to be normal.

The bed was all wrong somehow, and it felt like his body was floating above it and would fall at any moment.

He tried to move his right arm, but something was holding it down. Moving his other hand slowly, he felt his arm. Surrounding that arm, a cuff of some sort slowly inflated to the point of pain.

Jimmy pulled away and felt a stinging on his other arm. He touched a tubing that ran from his forearm to somewhere over his head.

"Oh, God, I'm still in this damn hospital. Still in this fucked-up situation where I can't do a damn thing without asking for help."

"Yes, that's right." A voice said. "You can't do a damn thing right without help, and I'm finally going to help you once and for all."

Jimmy whipped his head towards the voice he knew was his father's and opened his eyes. "What the hell are you doing here? Where's Mother? How the hell did you even get in my room?"

It hurt him to talk, but nothing and no one was going to stop him from demanding answers from this satanic beast sitting casually in his hospital room.

"What am I, doing here at this God-awful time of morning? What are you doing here? Pretending to be hurt, whimpering, and moaning like a whining old woman. I heard you murmuring in your sleep, and frankly, I've had enough of you and all your lies."

James Mattock Sr. took a sip from his coffee cup and placed it on a heavy hospital tray. He studied his son. "You're a poor excuse for a son or a man."

"Get out of my fucking room. Who are you to pass judgement on me? You, Daddy Dearest, are the embodiment of sadistic, twisted, prideful sins and a deranged example of what evil lives in this world."

Jimmy reached for the call button at his side to bring the nurses, doctors, or whoever to get this crazy man out of his room. To Jimmy's surprise, his eighty-year-old father moved remarkably fast to his side and stopped his hand.

"You can summon whomever you want after I finish my business with you. I have a few things I need to tell you first."

The senior Mattock squeezed Jimmy's hand in a painful grip until Jimmy had no choice but to release the device into his father's hand.

"I don't want to hear anything else from you," Jimmy sneered. "I didn't ask you to come here or come to my house. As usual, you pushed your way into my life, bringing nothing but discord. So don't try to convince me you are here out of the goodness of your heart. I know for certain you don't have one."

"You're nothing but an asshole. You're the one who brings the discord. And now you've driven your mother and me apart with all this foolishness."

"Me?! I haven't done anything except exist since day one. You're the one with ridiculous evil demands on top of outrageous commands. Frankly, I don't know how Mother has stayed with you this long. You're crazy, and have driven everybody else crazy too."

"Shut up and for once, listen to someone else instead of your own inflated ego."

"I can't believe you have the nerve to say that. No one, and I mean no one in this universe, has a bigger or more distorted view of themselves than you, Daddy Dearest."

Walking over to the window, James looked over the meticulous grounds of the hospital. He pulled his hand back from the blinds as the early predawn light tried to break through the darkest grey.

"Now, there's where you're wrong. And stop calling me 'Daddy Dearest.' It's demeaning, as I'm sure you meant it to be. I see myself exactly as I am. I know what I'm made of, and I know what lies deep inside you too."

"Just get out and leave me alone. You have never done anything that remotely showed kindness or compassion, so now is not the time to say you've started."

Jim turned his face away from his father while pulling the blankets up, and closed his eyes.

"You can stop feigning sleep. I'll only be here a few more minutes. Long enough for me to set you straight for the last time."

"You bastard, I don't have to listen to anything you—"

James Sr. laughed evilly. "That's where you're wrong again. I'm not the bastard. You are. And you will listen to me. If you would just stop mewling, like a kitten searching for its mama's teats, I'll tell you everything."

Jimmy opened his eyes and stared angrily at his father as if seeing a demon from hell. "What the fuck are you talking about? You need to get the hell out of my room before I call for the doctor."

"Your mother was brought to me already pregnant . . . with you. The worthless piece of shit that got her that way was long gone—"

"You lie! You lie, you liar! Why are you doing this? Get out now, or I'm going to throw you out."

Jimmy made a move to sit up in his bed, but the pain from his incisions stopped him in his tracks, and he moaned out loud.

"Lay your sorry ass back down and listen to me. I knew your mother's father from my early days when I was trying to start up my store. That was one mean son-of-a-bitch. Old man Charles Jadeaux was rich. Not just rich, but wealthy. The kind of money I always dreamed of.

"They had their own family float every year at Mardi Gras. The wealthy spend money like water. They came every year to Denver to spend time in the cool weather. And he had three daughters. Your mother was the youngest and apparently fancied herself in love with some piece of thrash."

"Why are you making up this wild story? What in the hell are you getting at?"

The senior Mattock sneered and continued as if his son had not asked any questions.

"Your mother let some lowlife knock her up, and her daddy about lost his ever-loving mind. Nobody was good enough for his precious baby girl and certainly not some street hustler."

James Sr. reached for his coffee cup and slowly brought it to his lips. He grimaced and continued with his tale.

The anger, the hurt, the mental abuse that had haunted Jimmy as a young boy seeped into his adulthood as he contemplated his so-called father.

All the pain, the sorrow, the vindictiveness, and the agony seemed to congeal into a new being as he listened to his father rant.

"This is some nasty coffee. I got it out of the machine in the waiting room before I coolly walked into your room. It's substandard, like everything else around me. But anyway, your mother's father needed my help to give his daughter's bastard some legitimacy, and I needed his money for my store. It wasn't a love match. It was purely a business transaction."

"You miserable fucker. You've never cared for anybody, not even my mother. She put up with you for all these years, and this is how you talk about her. You speak of her as if she was just a commodity, something to be used."

"Of course, she was. Much like your marriage to Jackie, if I'm not mistaken. They were both a means to an end. That's what women are for. But I digress. Your biological sire was a nothing, a nobody, and blood always tells. That's why you're the way you are."

Jimmy tried not to speak, but his fury overcame him. "That's enough. I don't want to hear any more of your cursed life stories. I never knew what real hate was until I came to know the real you. The only good thing about this is that it means you aren't my real father. Get out now, and never come back, or I can't be responsible for my actions."

The elder Mattock turned his back on Jimmy to toss his coffee cup away in the trash. He laughed cruelly at Jimmy's words as he studied the patient care info written on the board on the wall.

"You're the one who doesn't know hate, not the kind I have for you. In fact, the word 'hate' is much too mild. I had to look at a bastard, who I was supposed to raise and who your mother loved, and see some other man's seed. She had this old picture of her and that scoundrel. She hid it deep in her chest of drawers under her panties. She thought I didn't know, but I knew everything about her."

James Sr. gave a heartless laugh and continued. "You don't know hate until you have to do that. And you, the ungrateful mutt that you are, couldn't even live up to the plans I made for you. A total waste, just like your father. And then your weak mother tried to protect you. I couldn't stand to see you in my house, eating my food and wasting my time."

A fury like none he'd ever felt before, blasted through Jimmy's body. It started in his guts and boiled outward until it manifested into a physical entity. All he wanted was to give back as much or more hate and torture as had been given to him.

The entity seethed through Jimmy's mind, taking over any good sense he might have left. A blinding rage that wasn't foreign to him but had tripled in intensity took over his actions. And James "Jimmy" Mattock became the very thing he thought he was a victim of.

"All the years I wasted trying to turn you into a man who could at least follow in my footsteps. And what did I get?" his father said. "I ended up with you, a lying, deceitful, pitiful excuse for a man. A disrespectful piece of garbage."

As James Sr. rambled on, the entity that wore Jimmy's body slowly removed the blood pressure cuff from his arm. He looked to where he was connected to his IV and disconnected it, leaving a dangling line dripping onto the bed. He sat up, his body fighting back nausea and a near black out, and swung his legs to the floor.

"You have been the biggest thorn in my side. I hated you from the moment I laid eyes on you. You look just like that piece of shit that spilled inside your mother. You're nothing like your sweet sister. She has my genes, and it's plain to see."

Jimmy quietly picked up the heavy, empty, hospital tray while his father's back was still to him. As his father still spewing obscenities, started to turn around, Jimmy swung the edge of the tray as hard as he could, upside the head of the man he hated more than life itself.

The sound of metal against flesh mimicked that of a shovel hitting an over-ripe watermelon.

Jimmy swung again with massive strength, upside the other half of his father's head, knocking him around where he sagged from the first blow.

With a whimper, his father fell to the floor, bumping over the chair he tried to cling to.

With heaving breaths, Jimmy threw the tray on his father's prone body.

"No, old man. I do know that kind of hate. It's the only emotion I have left for you, and I want you to take it with you to your damn grave. You miserable old fucker, I hope you burn in hell."

The hospital door flew open, and a nurse stepped in. "What in the world is going on? I thought I heard a commotion in here. You're not supposed to have visitors at this hour."

The nurse came to a sudden stop as she saw a bleeding man on the floor and Jimmy standing over him, clutching his chest and breathing hard.

CHAPTER 14

MaryBeth and Bryan sat silently at the kitchen's dinette table and played with their breakfast.

Bryan had awakened much earlier and lay in bed brooding for some time. There was no good coming. He felt it all through his bones, chilling his body and his soul. The feeling tortured him so, and he'd dealt with it until he had no choice but get up and prepare some breakfast.

Jim was being ridiculous as usual, and now poor MaryBeth was caught up in her husband's hellish games. What a pair they made, Bryan and his mother-in-law. Both of them had picked the wrong person to love, to care for, and it was much too late to do anything good about it.

MaryBeth finally stopped picking at her food and spoke. "I called James's sister last night. We talked for quite a while."

"Really. Is she doing well? I remember her from Jim's and Jackie's wedding. She seemed like such a pleasant woman." Bryan stirred his coffee, wondering what other tidbits MaryBeth would drop.

"Yes, she's my darling. You know she used to be a model, but photography was always her passion. She's the apple of her father's eye—if any one is." MaryBeth brought an unsteady cup of coffee to her lips and smiled sadly.

"I remember. Jim would call her to check up on you guys from time to time."

"I told her some of what's going on here with James and all. She said if I needed her, she would fly in. She's in Paris right now." MaryBeth exhaled loudly and stirred her coffee.

"I tried to do what I thought was best for James, and Teresa. Their father was, and is, such a stern man. He never gave James a chance."

Bryan nodded his head in agreement with MaryBeth's statements. Again, he wondered what she was getting at.

"Is it time to go to the hospital yet?" MaryBeth picked up her fork and moved pieces of a waffle around on her plate.

"It can be if you want it to be. Jim's doctor said to come by around eleven. It's only eight, but I think we can do whatever we want. Oh, wait! That's my phone."

Bryan moved to the kitchen counter to grab his cell phone. "Hello."

"May I speak with Mr. Bryan Denveue?"

"This is Bryan Denveue."

"Mr. Denveue, this is Dr. Mannix from Northcentral Hospital. We have your husband admitted here, but there has been an accident involving Mr. Mattock's father."

"Oh no!"

MaryBeth looked up from her plate with wide eyes as Bryan rubbed his suddenly trembling hand over his face.

"Is Mrs. Mattock with you, sir?"

"Yes, she's here with me."

"Can you both please come to Northcentral this morning? I'll have more information when you arrive, Just come to Mr. Mattock's room."

"We'll be there as soon as possible. Thank you. Goodbye."

Bryan was visibly shaken as he ended the call and slumped against the countertop. He hesitated to speak, but had no choice but to.

"That was the hospital. There's been some sort of accident, and they want us to come as soon as possible."

"My goodness! Is James all right? What happened? What kind of accident can happen in a hospital? Is he hurt?"

MaryBeth hit Bryan with question after question as she wobblingly stood up from the table. She was so pale she looked as if she would faint at any moment.

"Jim is okay I think, but Mr. Mattock seems to have had some sort of accident. I'm not exactly sure of his status. Let's hurry and finish dressing, and then we can leave. Just hang on, and I'll get us there as quickly as possible."

"Mr. Denveue, Mrs. Mattock, if you will just wait here a moment, I'll get the doctor and security to speak with you."

"Thank you. You've been an immense help." Bryan nodded to the nurse as she stepped out of Jim's room. Bryan and MaryBeth had rushed to the hospital in a panic and had almost been involved in an accident themselves.

"Oh Bryan! I think I'm going to be ill. Whatever in the world is going on. For one minute, I didn't think we were ever going to make it here with all this crazy Atlanta traffic. And now James isn't even in the room. Why do you think everyone's being so cagey about what's going on?"

Bryan looked around the room before answering MaryBeth. He passed a hand over his mouth before speaking.

"I don't know. As far as traffic is concerned, that's just the usual metro traffic craziness. But as for the hospital staff, I don't know. I was told to come to Jim's room by a Dr. Mannix, but it looks like a fight broke out in here. I don't know what to make of all this either, but something seems wrong."

The door swung open, and accompanied by another man, the doctor they'd met the previous day came into the room. "Mr. Denveue, Mrs. Mattock, I'm sorry to have kept you waiting. First of all let me state that Mr. Mattock Jr. has been taken to get some x-rays and other tests done."

"Wait Dr. Floyd, what's exactly going on here?" Bryan asked. "When your staff called, they said Jim was all right, but his father was being treated."

Bryan looked at Dr. Floyd as he asked his questions, but his real attention was on the uniformed officer who'd entered the room with the doctor. "And exactly why is there a need for security?"

MaryBeth nodded her head in agreement with Bryan and said, "Yes, that's my questions also. "Where's my husband and what in God's name happened here?"

"Well, I was getting to that. It seems that your husband, Mr. Mattock Sr., somehow slipped into the hospital very early this morning, well before visiting hours. The best we can guess is that he came through the waiting room around four-thirty and proceeded to this room."

The officer spoke up and directed his answer to Bryan. "We have the camera footage from the hospital entrance, and it places Mr. Mattock Sr. coming through the doors around that time."

MaryBeth shook her head. "No, he wouldn't have done that. There was no reason for him to come here that early. You must be wrong."

"I'm sorry, Mrs. Mattock but he did come here, and apparently, some sort of altercation occurred between your husband and your son." Dr. Floyd took a deep breath and exhaled a long sigh.

"When Nurse Patrick, the overnight staff member, heard noise around five-thirty, she came to investigate. She reported seeing an older man lying on the floor and Mr. Mattock Jr. disconnected from his IV, standing over him in distress. She then called for assistance and tried to get your son back to his bed."

MaryBeth's knees buckled, and she leaned heavily against the hospital bed. "Oh my God! No. No, you can't be right. James, what have you done?"

"Dr. Floyd what are you trying to tell us? Please, can't you see you're stressing Mrs. Mattock out?" Bryan moved closer to MaryBeth and tried to steer her to the only seat in the room.

"No, Bryan, stop. I don't want to sit. I want answers. What exactly has happened to my son?"

"Well, to put it bluntly, your son has ruptured his incisions and been sedated again due to his hostile behavior."

MaryBeth stumbled back into Bryan's arms. "And my husband?"

"I'm sorry, but your husband has suffered severe blows to his head. He has massive brain swelling and we've put him in an induced coma. At this point, we can't be sure of his prognosis without further tests, but he's been placed on a respirator."

Dr. Floyd reached out to MaryBeth to take her hand in his. Bryan pushed the doctor's hand away and shouted, "You can't be serious! How in the world did this happen? Where are they? We want to see them right now."

The officer spoke from his stand by the door. "We'd also like to know exactly what happened. When the nurse alerted us, we found an unconscious Mr. Mattock Sr. on the floor, bleeding from head wounds. We tried to talk to Mrs. Mattock's son, but he became enraged and somewhat irrational. Dr. Floyd took him away for x-rays when he doubled over in pain after being questioned."

MaryBeth collapsed into the chair as Bryan yelled out, "This is preposterous! What are you trying to say?"

Bryan hugged MaryBeth as she sat slumped over, crying.

Dr. Floyd continued, "We're not trying to say anything but the facts as we know them right now. It appears that Mr. Mattock came to the hospital early this morning. He had some sort of interaction with his son. There's no one else seen entering the hospital except staff, and we have no reason to believe anyone else entered this room."

"This is a mess!" Bryan barked. "How can a person get hurt in the hospital?"

"As I said, he either fell and hit his head on a hospital tray or he was hit with the tray several times and collapsed on the floor. Either way, we have him in the ICU, and if you're ready, we can go see him now."

"Take me to my son right now," said MaryBeth. "I'm ready."

CHAPTER 15

Bryan hated to place the calls he knew would be life changing. "What do I tell them? What should I say?" He mumbled aloud to his cell phone.

He'd found a secluded spot in an empty waiting room on the ICU floor. His hands were damp now, and he tried to wipe one on his pants leg while holding the phone up to his ear with his other. He wished no one would answer so he didn't have to say what needed saying.

"Royce, hi. It's Bryan."

"Good morning, Bryan. What's up? Is there more news about Dad?"

"Well . . . yes, there is. Your grandmother and I are at the hospital, and it doesn't look good."

"What? What's happened to Dad?"

Bryan could hear the sudden tremor in Royce's voice. He breathed out loudly, trying to calm his own nerves.

"Uh, it seems there's been some sort of accident, and your grandfather has been admitted to the hospital with a severe head wound."

Bryan could hear Royce talking to Jessica. Bryan hated calling anyone this time of morning, but he hated more the message he needed to deliver.

"Royce, if you can please contact Chrystal and your mother. Tell them … tell them there's been an accident at the hospital and Mr. Mattock—Mr. Mattock is not expected to recover."

"Wait, Bryan. You've got to be kidding me. What in the hell is going on? I can't believe this."

Bryan looked around the empty waiting room to make certain he was alone. He spoke slowly and quietly into his cell phone.

"I understand your confusion. Your grandmother and I are just as confused. Your grandmother and I are just as confused. We've just come from seeing Jim and, Royce, your father is sedated for his own good. But I don't think he's in too bad of shape."

"Bryan, I don't understand. What happened to Dad?"

"Royce, I think Jim tried to kill his father."

NORTHCENTRAL HOSPITAL · 1:30PM

Bryan held a steadying arm around MaryBeth Mattock. She functioned as if on auto pilot--not responding to looks or touches, just breathing slowly in and out. The Mattock family had finally all made it to the hospital.

Royce had picked up his grandmother Sylvi and aunt Nancy from Ms. Sylvi's home after getting his grandmother's neighbor to watch Chrystal's kids. His mother and Eric had gone by Chrystal's house and brought her and Tyler with them.

Much speculation occurred in each car as each family member ran through what little information Royce had given them. They now all stood in a small conference room, where the hospital staff had offered to allow them to gather in private. They waited silently for Bryan to update them.

Bryan cleared his throat. "Thank you all for getting here so quickly. Please sit anywhere you want. I know this isn't how you wanted to spend your Sunday morning, or rather, afternoon." Bryan hesitated and wiped oily sweat from his face with a towel one of the nurses had given him.

Jackie spoke up from her place next to Eric. "Take your time, Bryan. It's all right. We just want to know what's going on."

While Bryan tried to collect himself, he helped a stiff MaryBeth to a chair. The other family members found seats and sat uneasily around the table.

Bryan avoided any one person's gaze as he looked up to the ceiling. "Mr. Mattock apparently came to the hospital very early this morning. He's seen entering the hospital at about four-thirty."

Chrystal exhaled a loud breath and shook her hair from her face. Tyler took her hand in his and held it gently as he spoke. "What are you trying to tell us? What did he do?"

MaryBeth came to life as if someone had flipped her "on" switch. "He came to do harm! That's what he's always done. He hated my son because he isn't Jimmy's father!"

MaryBeth suddenly stopped talking and wiped her eyes with a handkerchief, returning to her trance-like condition.

"What the hell?" Nancy looked sheepishly around the room, apologizing, and then finally settling her gaze on her sister's very surprised face.

Bryan continued with the story despite the bombshell MaryBeth dropped.

"Well, I don't know why he came, but I can assure you it was probably not with Jim's best interest at heart. The nurse on duty heard a commotion and came to investigate. She found Jim disconnected from his IV, standing over his father, who was lying on the floor."

Confusion broke out in the room as everyone started talking at once. Jackie managed to get her question heard over everyone else.

"Bryan, are you saying Jimmy hurt his father?"

"Well, the security officer on duty had to call the local police, and they're investigating. But from the condition of the room and the type of wounds Mr. Mattock sustained, it appears he either fell and hit his head, not likely, or yes, Jim hit him with a heavy hospital tray."

More confusing muttering danced around the room. Jackie shook her head and said, "That Jimmy is crazy. I knew something like this would happen one day. He has such a volatile temper and no self-control. I don't know what Mr. Mattock came to do, but apparently, Jimmy beat him to it. No pun intended."

Chrystal turned a confused face to Bryan as she stood up from her chair. "Bryan, can we talk to my father? Exactly what kind of state is he in?"

Eric asked another question as all eyes turned to him. "How is Mr. Mattock? What condition is he in?"

"My husband is in a coma and on life support. There appears to be brain damage due to a very nasty head wound. Like I said, he probably came to do my son harm and got exactly what was coming to him."

MaryBeth lapsed into silence again as every person in the room expressed shock and dismay.

Bryan didn't know if he could take any more surprises. His heart was racing and jumping about in his chest. MaryBeth had singlehandedly shut down the room.

It was amazing to think that Jim and his father suffered under the same misguided beliefs, ideals and even looks, but weren't related by blood. And to be so much alike with the same paternity issues repeating themself, while living very different lives.

Bryan didn't know if he even wanted to hear the rest of this story of the two Mattock men.

He fumbled with his hands on the tabletop. Wiping again at his forehead, he finally answered the room's occupants as Ms. Sylvi rocked back and forth in her seat, praying.

"From what we can tell," Bryan said, "Jim might have hit his father with the tray. MaryBeth and I tried to talk to Jim, but he wasn't very coherent. The more we asked him what happened, the more agitated he became. Finally, Dr. Floyd had to sedate him, and we were told to leave the room. But the doctor did say Jim's in stable condition and just needed some additional sutures to his incisions. He should recover."

Bryan rubbed his thinning hair and blinked tears from his eyes. "But I'm worried about his mental state. He kept mumbling something about a curse and demons. He made no sense at all."

Nancy pushed her chair back from the table. "Well, all I can say is that a demon came to town and got the hell beat out of him by the worst devil around. I'm sorry, Bryan and Mrs. Mattock, but it looks like they both got exactly what they deserved."

Jackie slumped back in her seat and shook her head sadly. She thought about all the misery these Mattock men had caused. And now, she thought, *I have even more news to tell them after looking at the message from the DNA testing site. It looks like it's gonna be another long, shitty day.*

NORTHCENTRAL HOSPITAL – ROOM 1032

James "Jimmy" Mattock awoke from a dream. It was so vivid that he wondered if it had actually occurred in real life. The colors had been crystal clear, the sounds like music to his ears. Even the taste of victory on his tongue lingered in his mouth.

He had looked down at a man lying in a hospital bed with all sorts of equipment hooked to his body, and he wondered about this man's identity.

As the dream progressed, Jimmy saw his father standing over the man in the bed and arguing with him. It suddenly occurred to him that the man was him.

That bastard had dared come to his room and caused his heart to burn. His father was telling him some wild story about his mother being a whore. Telling Jimmy how she was just a mean's to an end.

Jimmy remembered being so angry that he felt outside of himself. He wanted to hurt this crazy man so badly, but knew his mother probably wouldn't want him to do that.

As his father rambled on with his lies and deceit, Jimmy noticed more coldness had filled the room. He didn't know how he knew it, but his father was finally going to get what he deserved.

As Jimmy lay in his bed, someone picked up the heavy hospital tray and hit his father in the head so hard that spittle and blood flew from his mouth. The entity didn't stop hitting until the old man crumbled to the floor.

Jimmy laughed to himself as he thought, *yes that's a killing blow all right.*

To Jimmy's befuddled mind, it was just a dream.

But oh Lord, how he wished it was true, true, true.

AUTHOR'S NOTE

I know, I know. I'm leaving you with another cliff- hanger, but it will all come to a finale soon. Too many people have suffered with all the mayhem Jimmy Mattock and his father have put them through.

So, maybe, I just want to let them stew in their misery just a little bit more before their story reaches its conclusion.

Coming soon: *Crimson Gold*

Thank you for your support.

Barbara

THE BOOK THAT STARTED IT ALL

The Color of Your Tears
Mattock Family Saga
Book 1

When their son Royce came along, Jimmy completely forgot about their daughter Chrystal. Jackie remembered a little three year old Chrystal looking at her as she fed baby Royce, saying; "daddy loves him more, he don't piggy-back ride me no more." And Chrystal would cry big golden teardrops and Jackie's heart would break, because she knew it was true.

Maybe it was because Chrystal was conceived in desperation that made her so volatile, so unstable. Chrystal was so fussy as a baby that only Jimmy could manage her. She cried for whatever she felt she didn't have at the time. Nothing Jackie did for her was good enough.

Or was it because she wanted so badly to have a baby, thinking it would take away all the troubles in her marriage? She had done everything in her power to make a baby. And she was successful.

Royce on the other hand was conceived in joy and love. Royce was a good baby. A simple silly face would make him giggle and coo. She had never been in a better place in her life than when she carried Royce.

It brought Jimmy back home and he rubbed her back and stomach for her. He did everything he could to live up to his vows.

ABOUT THE AUTHOR

Barbara Combs Williams is a Georgia native. She is unapologetically old school and Southern grown.

She lives in the country with her husband of over forty years. She enjoys growing flowers, and watching the hummingbirds poke their beaks in the blossoms.

She hopes everyone can identify with her writing, and if you haven't yet, just wait, you will.

OTHER BOOKS BY THE AUTHOR

Crystal Clear - Mattock Family Saga Book 2

Soul Catcher, A Simple Maiden's Tale

Leighanne Abigail Hortense Packracker and Her Magical Growing Shoes, a children's story

In and Out Of the Mind Of -

Please see Barbara's website at:
www.BarbaraCombsWilliams.com